D1036170

"What do you want here, Adams?" Caulfield asked.

"Oh," Clint said, "I forgot to tell you."

He took the badge from his pocket and dropped it on the table.

"Aaron Caulfield, you're coming back to Denver with me to stand trial for murder."

Caulfield looked at his best gunhand, Stotter, sitting next to him.

"And what about me?" Stotter asked.

"I was going to bring you back, too," Clint said. "But after what you did to that woman last night, I think I'll just kill you. It'll be difficult enough to get him back to Colorado. I'd rather not try to bring you both back."

"And where are you gonna kill me, Adams?" Stotter asked. "In here?"

Clint looked around at the other people in the restaurant.

"No," he said with a cruel smile, "I can wait."

He stood up. "I just wanted to let you both know what was going to happen."

The Gunsmith turned and walked away . . .

**Look for the Western action series featuring
Longarm and Slocum, too!**

DON'T MISS THESE
ALL-ACTION WESTERN SERIES
FROM THE BERKLEY PUBLISHING GROUP

THE GUNSMITH by J. R. Roberts
Clint Adams was a legend among lawmen, outlaws, and ladies. They called him . . . the Gunsmith.

LONGARM by Tabor Evans
The popular long-running series about Deputy U.S. Marshal Long—his life, his loves, his fight for justice.

SLOCUM by Jake Logan
Today's longest-running action Western. John Slocum rides a deadly trail of hot blood and cold steel.

BUSHWHACKERS by B. J. Lanagan
An action-packed series by the creators of Longarm! The rousing adventures of the most brutal gang of cutthroats ever assembled—Quantrill's Raiders.

DIAMONDBACK by Guy Brewer
Dex Yancey is Diamondback, a Southern gentleman turned con man when his brother cheats him out of the family fortune. Ladies love him. Gamblers hate him. But nobody pulls one over on Dex . . .

WILDGUN by Jack Hanson
The blazing adventures of mountain man Will Barlow—from the creators of Longarm!

TEXAS TRACKER by Tom Calhoun
Meet J.T. Law: the most relentless—and dangerous—manhunter in all Texas. Where sheriffs and posses fail, he's the best man to bring in the most vicious outlaws—for a price.

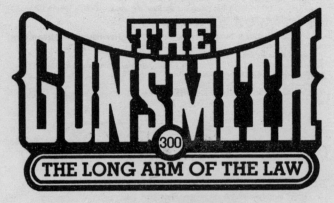

THE GUNSMITH

300

THE LONG ARM OF THE LAW

J. R. ROBERTS

JOVE BOOKS, NEW YORK

THE BERKLEY PUBLISHING GROUP
Published by the Penguin Group
Penguin Group (USA) Inc.
375 Hudson Street, New York, New York 10014, USA
Penguin Group (Canada), 90 Eglinton Avenue East, Suite 700, Toronto, Ontario M4P 2Y3, Canada
(a division of Pearson Penguin Canada Inc.)
Penguin Books Ltd., 80 Strand, London WC2R 0RL, England
Penguin Group Ireland, 25 St. Stephen's Green, Dublin 2, Ireland (a division of Penguin Books Ltd.)
Penguin Group (Australia), 250 Camberwell Road, Camberwell, Victoria 3124, Australia
(a division of Pearson Australia Group Pty. Ltd.)
Penguin Books India Pvt. Ltd., 11 Community Centre, Panchsheel Park, New Delhi—110 017, India
Penguin Group (NZ), Cnr. Airborne and Rosedale Roads, Albany, Auckland 1310, New Zealand
(a division of Pearson New Zealand Ltd.)
Penguin Books (South Africa) (Pty.) Ltd., 24 Sturdee Avenue, Rosebank, Johannesburg 2196,
South Africa

Penguin Books Ltd., Registered Offices: 80 Strand, London WC2R 0RL, England

This is a work of fiction. Names, characters, places, and incidents either are the product of the author's imagination or are used fictitiously, and any resemblance to actual persons, living or dead, business establishments, events, or locales is entirely coincidental.

THE LONG ARM OF THE LAW

A Jove Book / published by arrangement with the author

PRINTING HISTORY
Jove edition / December 2006

ISBN: 0-515-14228-X

JOVE®
Jove Books are published by The Berkley Publishing Group,
a division of Penguin Group (USA) Inc.,
375 Hudson Street, New York, New York 10014.
JOVE is a registered trademark of Penguin Group (USA) Inc.
The "J" design is a trademark belonging to Penguin Group (USA) Inc.

PRINTED IN THE UNITED STATES OF AMERICA

10 9 8 7 6 5 4 3 2 1

ONE

Clint Adams woke, rolled over, and found himself pressed up against a very shapely, somewhat plump ass. He adjusted, rolled over the rest of the way, and took a good look: blond and full-bodied with big, firm, pink-tipped breasts, smooth skin, and that plump butt. He remembered a night of very energetic, enjoyable sex.

He'd ridden into town yesterday, figuring on getting a quick drink and being on his way. Only it didn't happen that way. The town turned out to be much different from what he had imagined it would be at first glance. And the lady in bed with him had been a big part of that.

All he needed to do now was remember her name. . . .

When Clint Adams rode into the town of Contention, Colorado, he was struck immediately by how quiet it was.

Riding down the main street, Clint thought it looked like a normal enough small town. A hotel, two saloons, all the required businesses: mercantile, hardware, dress shop, gunsmith, and a couple of small restaurants. And apparently waiting for him halfway down the street the other necessity in a town like this: the law.

Clint reined Eclipse in as the sheriff stepped out into the street in front of him.

"Afternoon," the man said.

"Sheriff."

"Peters," the man said. "Sheriff Clement Peters. And who might I be talkin' to?"

"My name's Clint Adams, Sheriff."

"Adams," the man said. He was in his fifties, tall, and a little thick around the middle. It seemed pretty obvious that he had recognized the name.

"What brings you to our fair town, if you don't mind my askin'?" Peters said.

"I'm just passing through," Clint said, "on my way to Denver."

"Denver," Peters said, nodding. "Big city."

"Yes, it is."

"Got nothin' on us, though," Peters said. "We're pretty proud of our little town."

"Oh? Why's that?"

"Well, look at it," Peters said. "Or better yet, listen."

"It's quiet."

"Yer damned right it is," the lawman said. "Quietest town you'll ever want to see."

"Where is everybody?" Clint asked.

"Oh, they're around," the man said. "Lots of 'em in the saloons, I'd guess."

"That a fact? Good saloons?"

"That one across the street is the best," Peters said. "That's why we call it the Contention Saloon."

"Catchy name," Clint said.

"You plannin' on stayin' long, Mr. Adams?"

"I was thinking of having a drink and being on my way," Clint admitted.

"Well," Peters said, "maybe you'll find somethin' that'll change your mind, make you decide to stay awhile and enjoy what we've got to offer."

"I guess that's possible," Clint said.

"I'll just have to ask one thing."

"What's that?"

"We really don't look for trouble in Contention."

"I wasn't planning on bringing any with me," Clint said.

"That's good to hear, Mr. Adams," Peters said. "See, I know your reputation."

"I thought you might."

"And I have to tell you, I'm not impressed."

Clint grinned.

"That's okay, Sheriff," he said. "I'm not real impressed with it myself."

"Just so we understand each other."

"I think we do."

"Then I won't stand in the way of your gettin' that drink," Peters said, moving aside. "Have a nice day."

"Thanks, Sheriff."

Clint turned Eclipse and rode just across the street to the Contention Saloon.

TWO

As Clint entered the saloon, he saw that the sheriff was right. Middle of the day and the place was packed already. Most of the tables were full, including one in a corner that had a poker game going on. There were a few places at the bar and a couple of women working the floor. Nobody in particular paid attention to him when he entered, which, to his way of thinking, was good.

He walked to the bar and was immediately greeted by a smiling bartender.

"What'll ya have, stranger? And welcome to Contention."

"It's a friendly place."

"Yes, it is," the barkeep said. His smile revealed a row of even, if somewhat yellow, teeth. The evenness of them led Clint to believe that Contention had a good—and probably quiet—dentist.

"I'll have a beer," Clint said.

"Comin' up."

It was the fastest he'd ever gotten a beer, with a perfect head of foam that barely moved as the man put it down in front of him.

"How does that look?" the bartender asked.

"It looks just fine," Clint replied.

5

"Just let me know if you want anything else, stranger," the bartender said. "We aim to please in Contention."

"I'm starting to learn that."

With beer in hand Clint turned to survey the room again. The poker game was made up of four men. Two of them appeared to be town merchants from the way they were dressed. The third looked like a cowhand. The fourth man, however, was familiar to Clint. Not that he thought he knew him, but Clint knew his type. He was tall, lanky, and dark-haired, and when he looked at his cards he still kept his eyes on the room. There was a cigar in his mouth, the smoke spiraling up to the ceiling in a lazy fashion. His eyes caught Clint's and the two men nodded to each other, as if to say they had recognized each other.

At that moment Clint felt someone sidle up next to him, bumping into him firmly.

"Hello, stranger."

He looked down at the short, full-breasted blonde wearing a low-cut saloon dress.

"Hello."

"Are you looking for some company?"

"I might," he said. "I guess that would depend."

"On what?"

"On just how friendly a town Contention really is."

She smiled and said, "It can be pretty friendly. My name's . . ."

Rachel.

That was her name!

It came back to him as he replayed the previous day in his mind. It had been Rachel who had convinced him to get a room and stay in town for a while. She did it by being real friendly, offering to share his bed and not sassing for any money in return.

"Why would you do that?" he remembered asking her.

"Look around you," she said. "There's a shortage of

good-lookin' men in this town. Besides, you're a stranger, and we here in Contention like to treat strangers well."

And she did just that—and several more times during the night.

Clint pulled the sheet down so he could get a good look at her. If anything, she looked better in the daylight. Her skin was pale and smooth, almost seeming to glow in the sunlight that was streaming in through the window. He slid his hand down over her butt, first one round cheek then the other, then slid his finger down between them. She moaned, turned over, and reached up to stretch, which made her full breasts do interesting things.

"Jesus," she said, "I've never had a night like that."

"I'll bet you say that to all the boys, Rachel," he said, using her name so she'd know he remembered. He moved his hand up to her breast, just brushing the nipple with his palm. She was very responsive, and a shiver ran through her, causing goose bumps to appear on her perfect flesh.

"No, no," she said, "I mean it. That thing you do with your tongue? Ain't a cowboy in this town can do that to me."

She slid her hands up to cup her own breasts, bringing them together to trap his hand.

"Was I friendly enough?" she asked.

"Oh, yes," he said. "You proved the point that everyone here seems to be trying to hammer home. The sheriff, the bartender . . . nobody made the point quite as firmly as you have, though."

"Why, thank you, sir," she said. "I try my best."

She rolled over on her side and slid her hand down between his legs.

"And speaking of tryin' my best . . ."

She moved her hand down beneath his testicles, cupped them in her hand and fondled them, then moved up and took hold of his cock, which began to grow in her hand as she stroked it. Clint closed his eyes as her fingers glided over him. He felt the mattress shift, opened his eyes, and saw her leaning down over him. She ran her tongue over the head of his penis, wetting it, then slid her lips down over him and took him fully into her mouth.

She shifted around so that she was kneeling between his splayed legs. Holding him at the base with her thumb and forefinger her head began to bob up and down as she suckled him wetly, moaning in appreciation.

She got him good and wet, and when she thought he was ready, she released him from her mouth, swiveled around, and presented her butt to him. He spread her cheeks as she came down on him and he slid into her anus a little at a time until he felt her clench him. Slowly, she began to move her butt, gliding him in and out of her, her hands braced on the mattress. She groaned when he slid more deeply into her, moaned as he came out again, then repeated the process. He allowed her to control the pace, because he knew if this wasn't done right it could be painful for her. He hadn't done it this way with many women, but he wasn't inexperienced, either.

"Oh yeah!" she shouted. "That's it, baby—in and out, ooh, how does that feel?" He thought her voice was unnecessarily loud.

"It feels great," he said, but thought, Jesus, it feels amazing. She held him tightly in there, and yet he seemed to slide in and out of her easily. It was all the more erotic for him because he was able to watch her take his length all the way into her ass. He was starting to feel that buildup in his legs that told him he was preparing to explode, but before that could happen, the door of the room seemed to explode first, and men came pouring in.

THREE

Clint had to lean to the side to see around Rachel, whose majestic butt was in the air, blocking his view. She seemed oblivious to what was happening and continued to try to ride him as he reached for his gun belt, which was hanging on the bedpost. Finally, he pulled himself free of her, pushed her to the floor, and began firing as he threw himself off the bed on the opposite side.

His first bullet struck a man in the chest, dropping him in his tracks, and tripping the men behind him, whose own shots went wild into the floor and the ceiling. Clint got to his knees and fired again. One man took a bullet in the forehead, the other in the throat. Both hit the floor and did not move.

Effectively, the three men were piled up in front of the doorway, almost blocking it.

It was quiet for only a moment, and as Clint was about to speak to Rachel, the sound of shots came from down the hallway.

"What the hell—" he said, leaping to his feet. He grabbed his gun belt so he could reload if necessary, and ran out into the hall naked.

Down the hall, to the right, he saw several men, all with

guns in their hands, trying to get into another room. Then shots were coming from inside, and as he watched, two men staggered back into the hall and fell to the floor.

"Hold it!" he shouted, as another man was about to enter the room. He turned, saw Clint, and tried to bring his gun around, but Clint fired first, killing him instantly. There were now as many men piled up in the hall as in the doorway to his room.

He started down the hall as the shooting stopped, and abruptly a man burst into the hall. Like Clint, he was naked, gun in one hand, gun belt slung over one shoulder. They faced each other, guns pointed, and then relaxed when they recognized each other from the saloon. It was the man he'd seen playing poker.

"What the hell is goin' on?" the man asked.

"I'm not sure," Clint said. "You know any of these men?"

They walked back and forth in the hall, each regarding the other's pile.

"Him," the man said, referring to one of the dead men in Clint's doorway. "I played poker with him. Thought he was a cowhand."

Clint was looking at the men lying outside the other hotel room.

"This man was in the saloon . . . and so was this one."

He turned and looked into the room. On the bed, not bothering to try to hide her nudity, was a tall, lean brunette he had seen in the saloon. Her breasts were small and brown-tipped, and she stared at him with wide, unfrightened eyes.

He and the other man met midway between their rooms.

"You have a girl in your room," Clint said.

"So do you."

"Tell me, what were you doin' just before the men broke into your room?"

"What do you think?"

"And did she shout something out?" Clint asked. "Something very loud?"

"Now that you mention it . . . you think she was signaling those men?"

"I think you should get your woman and bring her to my room, and maybe we'll find out."

"Okay."

"By the way, I'm Clint Adams."

"My name's Slocum," the man said. "I've heard of you."

"Yeah, I recognize your name, too."

They stood silent for a moment.

"Nobody's coming to see what the shooting was about," Clint said. "Nobody's even opened a door."

"And where's the law?" Slocum asked.

"What's your girl's name?"

"Michelle."

"You go and get Michelle," Clint said. "And your pants. I'll meet you in my room."

Slocum nodded and headed for his room. Clint turned and entered his own. Rachel was back on the bed. Like the dark-haired girl, she was doing nothing to cover her naked body. Even in this situation, her buxom, bawdy appearance caused a stir within him.

"What happened?" she asked.

He didn't answer, grabbed his trousers, and pulled them on, then strapped on his gun belt. That done, he ejected the spent shells from his gun, reloaded, and holstered. Then he walked to the window to look out at the street. Just as quiet and empty as it had been the day before, when he rode in.

"Get inside!" he heard Slocum say, and the brunette came stumbling into the room, still naked. She staggered, struck the bed with her legs, and sat down on it. Both women on the bed, naked, made for an interesting sight. Rachel reached out and put her hand on Michelle's shoulder.

"What's goin' on?" she asked.

Slocum had also pulled on his trousers and strapped on his gun belt.

"That's what you ladies are gonna tell us," he said. He looked at Clint standing by the window. "Street?"

"Empty," Clint said. "Not a soul."

"Ain't right," Slocum said. "Just ain't right."

Clint came over to stand by the bed.

"Ladies," he said, "it's time you told us what's going on."

FOUR

"What are you talking about?" Rachel asked.

"What makes you think we know anything?" Michelle asked.

They both had identical wide-eyed, innocent looks on their faces. Of course, the fact that they were naked robbed them of some of their innocence.

"I'm getting a bad feeling about this," Slocum said.

"Me, too," Clint said. "Could the whole town be in on this?"

"Robbing strangers?" Slocum asked. "Maybe even killing them?"

They both looked at the women, who were suddenly looking less wide-eyed with innocence and more fearful.

"We didn't . . ." Rachel said.

"We don't want . . ." Michelle said.

"You girls better start talking," Clint said. "We don't take kindly to having folks try to kill us. We'd like to know the reason."

"We never . . ." Rachel tried again. "We don't want to do this. They make us."

"Make you what?"

"Distract you . . . men . . . who come to town."

13

"Distract them so they can be robbed?"

"Yes," Michelle said.

"And killed?" Slocum asked.

"Yes."

"The whole town?" Clint asked.

"Most of them," Rachel said. "There are others, like us, who are forced into it."

"And who's in charge?" Clint asked. "The sheriff?"

"Yes."

"No wonder he was so friendly," Clint said, "giving me all that talk about what a quiet town this is."

"You got that speech, too?"

Clint nodded.

"He know who you are?" Slocum asked.

"Yes," Clint said. "You?"

"Yeah."

"And apparently, he doesn't care," Clint said. "I guess he was telling the truth when he said he wasn't impressed."

"We've got to get out of here," Slocum said. "We can't hold off a whole town."

"We'll have to get to the horses," Clint said. He looked at the women. "Are our horses in the livery?"

"They should be," Rachel said. "They usually leave them there until . . . after."

"But they'll be guarded," Michelle warned.

The women were now being very cooperative, but that could have simply been because they'd been caught.

"What do we do with these two?" Slocum asked.

"We won't say anything," Rachel promised.

"Please don't kill us," Michelle said.

"We're not going to kill you," Clint said.

"We can't just leave them here and take their word they won't say anything," Slocum said.

"No, we can't," Clint agreed.

"B-but," Michelle said, "we're helping you."

"Helping us," Slocum said, "or sending us into a trap."

"We'll tie them up," Clint said. "Let's tear these sheets into strips."

"But—" Rachel started.

"Shut up, now," Slocum said. "Maybe Adams here won't kill you, but I won't hesitate."

Both women fell silent and stared at him.

They tore the sheets into strips, tied the women's hands and feet, and then gagged them. They also left them naked, lying face-to-face on the bed.

"Jesus," Slocum said, looking at the two women.

"I know," Clint said.

"Let's get out of here before I do something I'll regret."

Fully dressed, Clint and Slocum cautiously made their way down to the hotel lobby. When they got there it was empty, no one at all behind the counter or in sight.

"Bad, bad feeling," Slocum said.

"I know."

They moved across the lobby to the front door.

"There could be guns on every rooftop," Slocum said.

Clint nodded, scanning the rooftops with his eyes.

"And the doorway," he added.

"What about the back?" Slocum asked. "Think they'd have that covered?"

"That depends," Clint said.

"On what?"

"It all depends on whether or not they believed the six men they sent in after us could do the job."

Slocum nodded.

"I say they've got the front covered, but not the back."

"You want to bet your life on that?"

"I sure as hell ain't going out the front," Slocum said.

"I see your point," Clint said. "The back it is."

FIVE

"I told you this was a bad idea."

Sheriff Clement Peters looked over at his brother, Clark—the owner and bartender of the Contention Saloon. They were both in the sheriff's office looking out the window at the hotel across the street.

"If Adams and Slocum were dead, our men would be out by now," Clark said. "This was a bad idea. As soon as you found out who Adams was—jeez, Clem. Why would you want to try for both Slocum and the Gunsmith at the same time?"

"Because this is what we do, Clark," Clem said. "And we got 'em outnumbered. A whole town against two guns?"

"Two professional guns," Clark Peters reminded his brother. "We ain't professional guns, Clem. Ain't none of us as good as them two with guns."

"It don't matter."

"Our men are probably dead in there."

"That don't matter, either," the sheriff said. "They got to come out sometime."

"What if they come out the back?"

"Then they'll get to the livery and find a reception waitin' for them there."

"That why you got nobody watchin' the back?" Clark asked. "Because you want them to get to their horses?"

"I don't want them to get to their horses, Clark," the badge-toting brother said. "I just want them to go for their horses."

"You know," Clark said, "it may not be so bad if they did get to their horses and get out of here."

"And then what?" Clem asked. "You think those two won't send the law back here?"

"You're the law, Clem."

"I'm local," Sheriff Peters said. "Them two will send some federal marshals in here and we've had it. No, one way or another, little brother, we got to make sure that Clint Adams and Slocum never get out of Contention—not alive, anyway."

Clark Peters still didn't like it. He was nervous that maybe the ones not getting out of Contention alive might be him and his brother.

"Okay, come on," Clement Peters said.

"Where?"

"Outside," Clement said. "If this is gonna get done we're probably gonna have to do it ourselves."

"Jeez, Clem—"

"Quit your whinin' and come on!" Clement shouted.

SIX

"This ain't right," Slocum said.

They were standing behind the hotel, looking around, waiting for something to happen.

"Bad feeling again," Clint said.

"In spades."

"There should be someone back here," Clint said, "even if it's one person acting as a spotter."

Clint looked straight up the side of the hotel to the roof. The construction of the building was such that if someone wanted to look down at them he'd have to lean over to do it. Clint watched for several moments, but no one's head ever appeared.

"They want us to come out the back," Slocum said.

"And try for our horses," Clint said.

"They know by now their men failed, and are not coming out," Slocum said.

"So they're laying for us at the livery," Clint said, "wanting us to get that far."

The two men faced each other, trying to decide what to do. Clint didn't know how Slocum felt about his horse, but he had no intention of leaving Eclipse behind.

"I ain't leaving my horse here," Slocum said, as if reading Clint's mind.

"I agree," Clint said, "but maybe what we need to do is figure out a way to get them to bring the horses to us."

"And how do we do that?"

"There's only one person who could give that order."

"The sheriff."

"Right."

"So which way do we go to get out of here?"

Clint and Slocum both looked up and down, back and forth. It was obvious that there were back doors here that led to other buildings as well.

"I guess we ought to go through one of these other buildings to the front," Slocum said.

"And separately," Clint added. "You find a door you can get in through that way, I'll try this way. I'll see you out front."

"Right."

They split up, each checking doors. Clint found one that was unlocked, while Slocum located one that was easily forced. With a nod to each other, they entered their respective buildings.

"Where are we headed?" Clark Peters asked. "The hotel, or the livery?"

"I want to check the hotel first," the sheriff said.

Behind them were three of Peters's deputies. They were walking across the street, heading straight for the saloon. In the middle of the street, Sheriff Peters turned and waved at the gunmen he had stationed on the roof. The wave meant they were to get down off the roof, because they weren't needed anymore.

"What are you doin'?" his brother asked.

"They'll go over to the livery now."

"B-but, that leaves only five of us now."

"Against two men, Clark," Clement Peters said. "You don't think five against two is good odds?"

"Not when it's these two."

"You're too easily impressed, brother," the sheriff said. "Most of their reputation has been built up in bad dime novels. No one can do everything they're credited with doing."

"If they've only done half—"

"Not even half," Peters said, cutting his brother off. "Now just shut up about it. We're gonna check out the hotel."

Clint was in a feed and grain store that was obviously closed. Maybe one of the men he'd killed was the owner. Who knew? He worked his way to the front and looked out a window. He saw Sheriff Peters crossing the street to the hotel, four men trailing him, three with badges. He thought the fourth one was the bartender from the saloon.

He watched as the sheriff turned and waved up to the rooftops. Several men waved back and then disappeared. Clint hoped Slocum was watching, as he was. They had the option of letting the sheriff and his men enter the hotel and then heading for the livery, or they could stop the lawman and his deputies now. They were going to need the sheriff in order to get their horses.

Clint opened the door and stepped out, hoping Slocum was doing the same.

Slocum was in a hardware store, which was also closed. He made his way to the front and saw the same things Clint saw. He knew they'd have a hard time getting their horses without the sheriff, so he did indeed make the same decision Clint had made.

Take the sheriff and his men now.

He opened the door and stepped outside.

•   •   •

Clint and Slocum saw each other before the sheriff and his men did.

"Hold it, Sheriff!" Clint called.

The lawman looked over quickly at the sound of the voice and almost went for his gun when he saw who it was, but thought better of it.

"Adams. We, uh, were just comin' over to the hotel to see what all the shootin' was about. You wouldn't happen to know, would you?"

"I know exactly what happened, Sheriff," Clint said. "Six of your men are lying up in the hallway right now. They didn't quite get the job done."

"My men?" the sheriff asked. "I don't know what you mean. My men are right here."

"I see three deputies. What's the bartender doing here?"

"He's my brother."

"Interesting," Clint said.

"Let's take him, Clem," the bartender said. "Like you said, we got five and he's only one."

"Shut up, Clark."

"You're forgetting about me, ain't you?" Slocum called out.

The deputies looked over but the sheriff kept his eyes on Clint.

"That would be Mr. Slocum, right?"

"That's right."

"Are you sayin' that some men tried to kill both of you? In my town? That's shockin'."

"Drop the act, Sheriff," Slocum said. "Your brother gave you away, didn't he?"

Clint saw the look on the sheriff's face change from something benign to rage, and then back again.

"My brother's an idiot, gentlemen," he said. "He doesn't know what he's sayin'."

"Hey!" Clark protested.

"Shut up, Clark!" Sheriff Peters snapped.

"Okay, here's the deal, Sheriff," Clint said. "Slocum and I want our horses. We're going to leave your fair town."

"Well, go ahead, then. Your horses are over at the livery. Go and get 'em and be gone, with my blessing."

"No," Clint said. "We've got a better idea. We want you to send your men over to get the horses for us."

"And why's that?"

"Because while we've got you here, nobody's going to try to kill us again."

"You think holdin' me here's gonna keep you safe?"

"We're banking on it."

"I think you got the wrong idea—"

"Either send your men for the horses," Clint said, "or have them go for their guns—and you, too, Sheriff."

"Adams—"

"Let's make a decision," Clint said, "right now."

SEVEN

Clint thought for sure the sheriff would make the right decision, despite the fact that he and Slocum were outnumbered five to two.

He was wrong.

He saw it in the man's eyes before he even made a move. The lawman drew, figuring his deputies and his brother would draw with him. He was only partially right.

As the sheriff drew, Clint did not bother to pay any attention to Slocum. The man had a reputation and if it was true he'd be doing his part.

Behind the sheriff, the deputies drew, two turning toward Slocum, the other moving toward Clint and his boss.

Clint had a problem, though. The sheriff was intent on killing him, but he wanted the lawman alive to help them get their horses. Luckily, all of the men were slow—very slow.

Clint drew and killed the deputy with one shot. He put the bullet right through the star on the man's chest, because the sheriff and his deputies had no right to be wearing those badges.

Next he shot the sheriff in the right shoulder, paralyzing his gun hand and causing the weapon to fall to the ground.

Behind him, Slocum had dispatched the other two deputies with a shot each.

Clint looked at the bartender next.

"No, no, no," the man shouted, thrusting his hands in the air. "I'm just a bartender, not a gun hand."

Slocum stepped into the street, ejecting empty shells and reloading as he approached Clint.

The sheriff was down on one knee, holding his bleeding shoulder and alternating between giving Clint a look of hatred, and his brother one of disappointment.

"Drop your gun," Clint told the bartender.

The man obeyed.

"If you'd drawn we coulda had them," the sheriff said to his brother.

"If he'd drawn," Clint said, "he'd be dead, too, Sheriff."

"I ain't dead," the lawman said.

"That's only because we need you," Slocum said. He pressed the barrel of his gun to the man's temple. "Of course, if you want to die . . ."

"No, no!" Clark Peters shouted. "Don't kill 'im."

"Don't beg for my life, Clark," Peters said with a snarl. "I ain't afraid to die."

"No?" Slocum asked. He removed the gun from the man's head, walked to his brother, and pressed it to his temple. "How about now? You afraid to have him die? Your little brother?"

Clark's eyes widened and he looked at his brother, his eyes imploring.

"Clem?"

"Shit," Clem Peters said. "Okay, what the hell do you want?"

Clint and Slocum took the sheriff and his brother into the hotel lobby. Clint found a towel behind the desk and gave it to the lawman to hold against his wound.

"Oh," he said, "one more thing." He grabbed the badge

and tore it from the man's chest. "You don't deserve to wear this." He tossed it on the front desk.

"What are you gonna do now?" Peters asked.

"We're going to leave town," Clint said. "Your brother is going to go to the livery and get our horses. If he's not back in the allotted amount of time with them, you'll be dead."

"You wouldn't kill me," Peters said to Clint. "I'm un-armed, and there's nothin' in your rep—"

"I'd do it," Slocum said, cutting him off. "In a minute."

Peters looked at Slocum, then said, "Yeah, I believe you would."

"Then tell your brother what to do," Clint said.

"Clark," Peters said, "go and get their horses."

"Sure, Clem."

"Don't tell the men at the livery what's going on," Clint instructed. "Just tell them your brother sent you for our horses."

"Maybe I better go with him," Slocum said. "Just to be sure he doesn't take off on one of our horses."

"He won't do that," Clem Peters said, clutching the bloody towel to his shoulder. "He'll do what I tell him to do."

"Once he gets back with the horses and we're gone," Clint said, "you better think about moving on, too, Peters. We'll be sending some federal law back here to clean things up."

"I know that," Peters said with a scowl. "Didn't think this deal would last forever."

"Maybe the town will even grow with you out of the way," Clint commented.

"Without me this place will wither and die," Peters said. "Mark my words."

"Well, that's too damn bad," Slocum said. "Like I give a good goddamn what happens to this place."

Peters glanced over at Slocum, then looked away. He couldn't look the man in the eye.

"Go and get those horses, Clark," he said. "And for chrissake, don't fuck it up!"

EIGHT

When Clark Peters returned twenty minutes later, leading both horses, he didn't bring good news with him.

"I couldn't stop them, I swear," he told Clint and Slocum as they stepped out to greet him.

Trailing along behind him were five more men, all carrying guns. Some of them had probably been on the roof, and the others stationed at the livery.

"My men are loyal," Clem Peters said from behind them.

"Loyal enough to get you killed?" Slocum asked.

"Even if you ride out of here you won't get far," Peters said. "They'll come after you."

But Clint noticed something. The men were looking at the bodies on the ground, concern on their faces.

"Try goin' upstairs," Slocum told them. "You'll find six more of your friends there."

The men all exchanged glances, then backed away a bit to talk among themselves.

"Looks like your loyal men are having second thought, Peters," Clint said.

But as Clint and Slocum turned they saw Peters, bloody

arm hanging, coming out from behind the front desk with a gun in his left hand.

"Gun!" Slocum yelled.

Both men drew and fired twice each. All four shots hit the now ex-lawman in the chest, driving him back onto the desk, which collapsed beneath his weight.

"Clem?" Clark called from outside.

Clint turned and stopped the man from entering the hotel.

"He didn't give us any choice," he told him.

"Your brother had a death wish," Slocum said.

The man stepped around them and entered the hotel lobby. Clint and Slocum again ejected spent shells and reloaded. They wanted to be ready just in case the five men outside turned out to be extremely loyal.

Clint stepped down into the street to retrieve the two horses and led them over to the hitching post in front of the hotel door. Slocum came over to accept his horse's reins.

"If we mount up and ride out real slow they might not react," Clint suggested.

"On the other hand," Slocum said, "if we mount up and ride out hell-bent for leather we'll catch them all flatfooted."

"I don't think they'll follow," Clint said. "Not when they see that their boss is dead."

But at that moment Clark Peters, who had acquired a backbone from somewhere, came out with a gun in his hand, shouting, "They killed my brother! Get them!"

Clint wondered just how many damn guns were hidden around the hotel lobby as he drew his weapon and shot Clark Peters in the chest. The force of the bullet drove the man back inside.

Slocum and Clint both turned to face the other five men, all of whom seemed unsure about what to do.

"Slap leather or go home," Slocum told them.

One by one, they peeled off and walked away, until they were all gone.

Suddenly, the street started to fill with people, closing in around them. Clint was worried for a moment—how could they fend off an entire town?—but then he noticed there were no weapons in evidence. Men, women, even some children converged on them, and then a man stepped forward.

"Are they dead?" he asked. "The sheriff and his men?"

"The sheriff and most of his men," Clint said. "The others just sort of . . . went away."

And all of a sudden the people were cheering and slapping Clint and Slocum on the back.

"We can't thank you enough for gettin' rid of them varmints," somebody said.

"They had us under their thumb for two long," a woman said. "Our men couldn't do nothin'!"

The crowd didn't seem to be bothered by the dead bodies in the street. In fact, several men went into the hotel and carried each of the brothers out in turn, tossing them into the street, as well.

A party atmosphere prevailed as Clint and Slocum mounted their horses and started out of town.

"You know," Slocum said when they were outside of town, "we left them women tied up, face-to-face . . . naked."

"Don't remind me," Clint said. "I might go back."

"Yeah," Slocum said, "it was quite a sight. Well, where you headed after this?"

"Denver," Clint said. "Going to stop and see some friends. You?"

"Me, I'm just gonna mosey a bit," Slocum said. He put his hand out. "It was a real pleasure fighting alongside you."

Clint took the hand and shook it.

"Same here. I'm surprised we haven't crossed paths before."

"Well, now that we have," Slocum said, "we probably will again."

He turned his Appaloosa and headed south. Clint watched him go and wondered how many other men he could have held off a whole town with.

NINE

Denver

There were only a few places in the country Clint Adams ever felt truly at home. The Denver House Hotel in Denver was one of them. The owners were welcoming every time he showed up there, and always had a room for him. Amazingly, it was usually the same room.

After the events in Contention, his first few days in Denver were very relaxing. He had seen some shows, met a couple of very nice ladies, and eaten some great meals, but he was still waiting for his friend Talbot Roper to return to Denver so he could visit with him.

Roper was the ex–Pinkerton operative who had opened his own office in Denver years ago, and was generally considered to be one of the best private investigators in the country.

Clint had stopped at his office and been told by his secretary—a new girl he didn't know—that Roper would be back in town by the end of the week. Roper's taste in secretaries still ran to the young and lovely, and naturally, Clint invited her out for dinner. Two nights later they were in bed in his hotel room. Her name was Nancy, a tall, slender redhead who made up in eagerness what she lacked in experience.

This morning, however, he was in bed with a woman named Lola. He had met her at the theater and they'd hit it off instantly—so well, in fact, that she took him home with her that night. A busty brunette in her late thirties, twice widowed, and twice divorced—every time to a rich older man—she had both eagerness and experience, and used them both with equal talent.

When he rolled over, Lola was lying with her back to him. They'd agreed last night to come to his hotel rather than going to her house. Seeing her lying there made him think, just for a moment, of Rachel, the blonde in Contention. The only similarity between them was that exquisite, round butt.

He ran his hand over both cheeks, then pressed himself up against her so that his penis, as it hardened, crawled up the deep crack between her butt cheeks.

"Mmm," she said, reaching behind to touch him, "you sure know how to wake a gal up."

He reached around in front of her to touch her and found her instantly wet, so it was a simple thing to slide his cock up between her legs and into her.

"Oooh," she moaned, "my God, you fill me up, Clint Adams."

She moved her butt then, pressed it back against him, opening her legs and taking him deep inside her. They moved together that way, him gliding in and out of her sweetly, reaching around to cup her breasts or pinch a nipple or simply to stroke her.

He felt her begin to tremble then, the preamble to her orgasm. Already he knew that hers were so violent and pleasurable that she sometimes came close to passing out. He'd never known a woman to enjoy her pleasure so much.

As she began to buck wildly against him, he wrapped his arms around her and continued to ride her. In fact, he rolled both of them over so that he was on top of her, her ass checks pressed firmly against him. As her tremors began to fade, he drove himself in and out until he exploded inside her, which set her off on another pleasurable journey.

Moments later she was on her back, her arms above her head. When she brought her arms down again her breasts actually flattened a little, each falling to the side. Her full breasts were not as high as they once had been, the weight of them dragging them down just a bit, but he found it extremely attractive. He leaned over and kissed each penny-brown nipple in turn, giving each a lingering lick.

"Ohh," she said, shivering, "don't get me started again."

"Why not?" he asked, sliding his hand down over her belly. "What else have we got to do today?"

His fingertips had just delved into the tangle of black hair between her legs when there was a knock on the door.

"Damn," he said.

"See?" she said. "Somebody's on my side. I need rest after last night and this morning. Remember, I'm an old girl."

"Nothing old about you, my girl," he said, swinging his legs to the floor. She rolled over onto her side, once again presenting him with her butt, and he slapped it enthusiastically.

"Ow!"

He pulled on a pair of trousers and went to the door in the sitting room of the suite.

"Yes?"

"Mr. Adams?" a voice called. "It's Danny, the bellboy?"

Clint opened the door. Danny the bellboy was, indeed, a boy, whereas many of the bellboys in the Denver House had been there so long they could no longer be called that. This one, on the other hand, looked all of sixteen.

"What is it, Danny?"

"Somebody downstairs to see you."

"Tell them to go away."

"It's somebody with a badge."

"What kind of badge?"

"Deputy federal marshal."

"Oh, that kind." He wondered if this had anything to do with Contention. He had reported everything that had happened in that town to the marshal's office when he got to Denver.

"What does he want?"

"To talk to you, he says," Danny replied. "Right away."

"All right," Clint said. "Have the man wait in the restaurant. Tell him he can have breakfast with me, if he hasn't eaten already."

"All right, sir."

Clint found a coin in his pocket and gave it to the boy.

"Thank you!"

He closed the door and went back into the bedroom. Lola had rolled herself up in the sheet, so that he could no longer see her naked flesh.

"Covering up?"

"I need to keep you off me," she said, pouting. "A girl's got to get some rest."

"Well, now you can get some. I have to go downstairs."

"Now?"

"Yes." He looked around for a shirt.

"For how long?"

"I don't know," he said. "Apparently, there's a lawman down there wants to talk to me."

"Well," she said, "don't stay away too long." She unwrapped the sheet and opened it to show him her full breasts, brown nipples, furry black thatch, smooth, muscular thighs, and round, firm butt. "I don't need that much rest."

"You're a little bit of a bitch, aren't you?" he asked as he left.

TEN

When Clint got to the hotel's restaurant—one of the finest in the city—he found a tall mustachioed gentleman in a brown tweed suit waiting for him. As he approached, the man was tucking away a turnip watch into his vest pocket.

"Sorry to keep you waiting, Marshal," Clint said.

"No trouble," the man said, standing. He extended his hand. "Deputy Marshal Custis Long."

"Deputy. Clint Adams."

They sat down and a waiter came over.

"Breakfast?" Clint asked.

"That's okay, I ate. I'll have some coffee, though."

Clint ordered steak, eggs, and coffee.

"What can I do for you, Deputy?"

"I work for Marshal Billy Vail's office here in Denver. You spoke to him earlier this week, something about a whole town trying to kill you and a fella named Slocum?"

"I did tell him about that, yeah," Clint said. "Is there a problem?"

"Not with what happened, but I do need your help with something else."

"Wait a minute," Clint said, snapping his fingers. "You're the one they call Longarm."

"I am, yes," Longarm said, "but I'd prefer to be called Deputy, if you don't mind."

"No problem," Clint said. "Believe me, I understand completely."

"You being the Gunsmith," Longarm said, "I thought you would."

"Okay," Clint said, "now that we've got that settled, what is it you need my help with?"

At that moment the waiter interrupted and poured coffee for both of them.

"Thanks," Clint said.

"I'll be back with your steak and eggs, sir."

Clint nodded.

"Maybe you can get it out before he comes back," Clint said.

"I need to leave Denver and track down a man named Aaron Caulfield."

"I don't know him."

"He's a vicious killer," Longarm said. "He and his gang have already killed several families—"

"Families?"

"They hit ranches," Longarm explained. "Rob them, kill the family, burn down the house . . . They have their way with the women first, if there are any. Young girls, too."

"Why do you need my help? Doesn't your office employ enough deputies?"

"Normally, yes," Longarm said, "but we've got a shortage of deputies right now."

"Why's that?"

"Because Caulfield and his gang killed two already."

"And that makes you short?"

"Well . . . some of the others have turned in their badges rather than go after Caulfield and his gang."

"How many in the gang?"

"From all reports," Longarm said, "and from evidence

left at the scenes, could be anywhere from twelve to twenty."

"Can't your Marshal Vail hire more men?"

Longarm sat back. His coffee cup sat on the table in front of him, untouched.

"Seems we got a shortage of them, too."

"Men willing to wear a badge and go after this gang?"

"That's right."

"Denver's a big city, Deputy," Clint said. "There's got to be somebody here who will go with you."

"I'm hoping there is, Mr. Adams." Longarm sat forward again and said, "You."

ELEVEN

"Wait a minute," Clint said. "Let me get this straight."

The waiter had brought his steak and eggs, giving him time to consider Longarm's words.

"You want me to go with you to track down a gang of twelve to twenty killers?"

"Right."

"And there would be how many of us?"

"Two," Longarm said. "Just you and me."

"And if I don't go with you?"

"I'll have to go alone."

"Why would you do that?"

"It's my job."

Clint cut a hunk of steak, picked up some eggs, popped them into his mouth, and chewed thoughtfully.

"You're bluffing," he said, finally, gesturing with his fork.

"In what way?"

"You wouldn't go alone."

"You don't know me very well."

"I don't know you at all, Deputy," Clint said. "And you don't know me. Why would you ask me to go with you?"

"Marshal Vail told me you were in his office," Longarm

43

said. "He told me the story of Contention, and what you and John Slocum did."

John? That was Slocum's first name?

"And?"

"I was impressed," Longarm said. "If the story you told was true, you stood off a whole town."

"Not a whole town," Clint said. "Just a bunch of men with guns."

"How many?"

"I don't know . . . over a dozen."

"See? So you've done this already."

"That was self-preservation," Clint said, chewing some more. "If we hadn't gotten out of that town we would have been dead."

"Still," Longarm said, "it was impressive."

"Slocum's a good man," Clint said. "Why not ask him to help you?"

"I don't know where he is, and you're right here."

"Deputy—"

"I tell you what," Longarm said, pushing his chair back and standing up. "Think it over. I'm leaving in the morning. I'll come by and see if you're ready to go. If not, no hard feelings."

He picked up his hat.

"Enjoy your breakfast, Mr. Adams. Thanks for listening to me."

"Deputy," Clint said, "how can you even think about tracking down twenty men by yourself?"

"I look at it this way," Longarm said, putting on his hat, "they'll be easy to track."

Clint thought it was completely unfair of Deputy Marshal Custis Long to put him in this position. Why should he feel guilty saying no to a man he didn't even know? Especially when he was asking him to go on a suicide mission with him.

No, he wasn't going to do it.

He waved the waiter over.

"Can you find me a newspaper?"

"Of course, sir."

He needed something to take his mind off the deputy's offer while he finished his breakfast.

The waiter returned with a copy of *George's Weekly*.

"Thank you."

"More coffee, sir?"

"Yes," Clint said. "Another pot."

"Coming up."

Clint set the newspaper down next to his plate, picked up his knife and fork and cut another hunk of steak. He was about to put it in his mouth when he saw the headline on the front page.

CAULFIELD GANG STRIKES AGAIN, MURDERS FAMILY OF FIVE!

He went on to read the story. The family's name was Dupont and consisted of a father, a mother, two daughters, and an infant son. According to the report, the daughters were eleven and thirteen, which would have made the mother fairly young as well—especially since she'd had an infant son. The story went on to describe how the gang had apparently passed the females around, raping them until they were dead. The males—both the father and the infant—had been shot in the head. The ranch had been burned to the ground.

"A terrible thing," the waiter said.

Clint looked up. The man had returned with the second pot of coffee, and was reading over his shoulder.

"Something's got to be done about them," the man went on.

"What's your name?"

"Walter, sir."

"Walter, if the marshal came to you and asked you to help ride these men down, would you do it?"

"No, sir."

"Why not?"

"I have a wife and two daughters," the man said.

"How old are your girls?"

"Teenagers, sir. One of them is going to college next year."

"Don't you sympathize with these families?"

"Yes, sir, I do," Walter said, "but I have to watch out for my own family first." He put the pot down on the table. "Anything else, sir?"

"No," Clint said. "Thank you, Walter."

The waiter left and Clint put down his knife and fork. He wondered if Longarm had somehow gotten the waiter to bring him this newspaper. Then again, any newspaper Walter brought would probably have the story in it.

Inside, on page six, he found a column by the newspaper's editor, writing about the ineptness of the marshal's office in not being able to catch this gang. It went on to say that two marshals had been killed and several had resigned in the wake of those murders.

So Longarm had not been exaggerating.

Clint closed the newspaper and set it aside. He looked down at his meal, then picked up his knife and fork, determined to finish. He'd think further on the matter after that.

Chief Marshal Billy Vail was pink-cheeked, balding, and chubby, but he had once been a fearful lawman in his own right, serving with both the Texas Rangers and as a deputy marshal. Now he sat in his office on Colfax Avenue and dispatched younger men to do the dirty work.

He stared across the desk at Longarm.

"So what did he say, Custis?"

"He said no, Billy," Longarm replied. "What else would a man in his right mind say?"

"You expected him to say no?"

"Of course," Longarm said. "The man's not an idiot."

Vail shook his head.

"Damn it! Those varmints are going to keep getting away with murder."

"No, they're not, Billy," Longarm said. "I'm going to stop them."

"Alone?"

"If I have to."

Longarm stood up.

"I'll be leaving at first light."

Vail regarded his best deputy for a moment, then said, "If I've ever met a braver man, Custis, I don't know when it was or who he was."

"Don't go soft on me, Billy," Longarm said. "Next thing I know Henry'll be saying something nice to me."

The marshal's clerk was Henry, a pasty-faced young man who manned the front office, and did not get along with Longarm at all. The two mixed like oil and water.

"I don't think things will get that bad, Custis," Vail said.

"Let's hope not, Billy," Longarm said. "Let's hope not."

TWELVE

It was several hours later when Clint was back in his room that a knock came at the door. Lola had left, so he thought it might be her coming back. When he opened the door there was a portly, pink-cheeked man standing there wearing a marshal's badge. They had met days earlier when Clint reported the incidents taking place in Contention.

"Marshal," he said.

"Mr. Adams. Mind if I come in?"

"Be my guest."

He stepped back to let the lawman enter, then closed the door and turned to face him.

"Something to drink? I think I can offer you—"

"That's all right," Billy Vail said, removing his hat and running his hand over his balding pate. "I just came here to talk."

"About Custis Long?"

"Exactly."

"Have a seat."

They each lowered themselves into overstuffed armchairs, ignoring the equally plush sofa.

"I understand Deputy Long came to see you."

"He did."

"And you turned him down."

"I did," Clint said, "and I'm sure he knew I would."

"Oh, he knew," Vail said. "His exact words were, 'The man's not an idiot.'"

"Then he knows me better than I know him after our short meeting," Clint said.

"Nobody knows him very well," Vail said, "not even me, and I probably know him best."

"So you're here to ask me to go with him?"

"Yes."

"You know we'll probably be killed."

"I know that he has a better chance of coming back alive if the Gunsmith is with him."

"And what of my chances?"

"Better with him than without him."

"Better yet if I don't go," Clint said. "And he shouldn't go, either."

"Oh, he'll go. It's his job."

"It's not mine."

"Shall I offer you money, then?"

"That would be insulting."

"A badge, then?"

"I don't need or want to wear a badge."

"Then let me just appeal to your sense of—"

"Of what? Fair play? Twenty against one, or two? How fair is that, Marshal?"

"Mr. Adams," Vail said, "I believe that you and Custis can get the job done."

"The job being?"

"Bring back Aaron Caulfield."

"Just Caulfield? Not his men?"

"He's the head," Vail said, "and they are the body. Cut off the head and the body dies."

"And you'd settle for that?"

"They'll get theirs eventually," Vail said. "My number-one priority is to put Aaron Caulfield away or, better yet, watch him hang."

Well, this was a different kettle of fish. Bring back one man, not twenty, not twelve.

"He'll still have his men around him, though," Custis countered.

"Not all the time," Vail said. "You'll catch him alone, sooner or later. All you got to do is find him, and watch him."

Clint put his head back and stared at the ornate ceiling above them. It must have taken a lot for this man to leave his office and come here asking for his help. And it must have taken just as much for Longarm to have asked.

"I realize this will be a real test of your mettle," Vail said, "not to mention Deputy Long's. If we did not have such a shortage of able men I wouldn't ask—"

Clint held up his hand to cut Billy Vail off.

"Just stop trying to sell it, Marshal," he said. "Let me think a minute."

"Of course."

Clint stood up and walked to the window and stared down at the street. He'd come to Denver for some time out from a hectic life, but when did that ever really happen? Just like the events in Contention, trouble seemed to seek him out, usually in the guise of someone who needed help. He never would have thought a call would come from badge toters like Billy Vail and Custis Long.

"Where is this crazy deputy of yours now?" he asked Vail.

"I'm not sure," Vail said. "He might be in his room, or he could be at the library."

"The library?"

"He likes to read." Vail took out his watch and checked it. "In fact, I'm almost sure he'll be there. It's near the end of the month, which means he'll have no money for gambling."

"All right," Clint said. "I'll go and talk to him, and make my final decision after that."

"That's all I ask, Mr. Adams," Vail said, standing.

The two men shook hands and Clint opened the door for him. Vail hesitated in the doorway.

"There's just one thing," he said.

"What's that?"

"In the event you do agree to go with him, I'll need you to wear a badge."

"I'll tell you what," Clint said, "in the event I decide to go, you give me a badge. What I do with it will be my business."

Vail hesitated, then nodded and said, "Fair enough."

As the man left, Clint thought how he'd had enough of wearing a badge in his younger days. He'd found folks just didn't appreciate what went into toting a star. Besides, it wouldn't be fair for him to wear one when a fellow like Longarm had spent all these years behind one, earning the right to wear it.

Clint changed his clothes, putting on something more appropriate to the streets of Denver, and the library. It wasn't the three-piece tweed suit that Longarm had been wearing, but it would do.

He took out his .32-caliber Colt New Line and tucked it in his belt at the small of his back. The hideout gun had saved his life more than once and was a favorite of his.

Dressed and armed, he left his room and headed for the Denver Library, an establishment he didn't recall ever having been to before.

THIRTEEN

Clint was inside the Denver Library for two minutes when he realized what the appeal could be for Longarm—aside from the books. He spotted several lovely ladies working there, one of whom was deep in conversation with the deputy at that moment. It wasn't hard to figure out what they were talking about, because the young woman was blushing furiously.

"Deputy," Clint said, coming up alongside them.

It was clear Longarm had spotted him as soon as he'd entered, for the man showed no surprise at his appearance.

"Adams. This is Mary Lou."

"Hello, Mary Lou."

"Can I help you find a book?" she asked, her pretty green eyes all wide and innocent.

"No," Clint said, "actually, I came here to talk with the deputy."

"Oh, well, then I should get back to work," she said. "See you next time, Custis."

"As soon as I get back to town, Mary Lou."

As the girl flounced off, Longarm turned to face Clint.

"You're making a date for when you return from tracking down the Caulfield gang?"

"I believe in the power of positive thinking," the deputy said. "What can I do for you?"

"Your boss came to see me."

That surprised Longarm.

"Billy Vail came to see you? At your hotel?"

"That's right," Clint said. "Seems he's worried about you getting yourself killed."

"That's right nice of him," Longarm said, "but this ain't no different from any other time. Every time I leave Denver there's a chance I won't be coming back."

"Well, apparently he thinks the chances are even better this time. After all, you'll be going up against twenty men."

"Or twelve."

"Twelve, fifteen, twenty, that's still a lot for one man to face."

"Haven't you heard?" Longarm asked. "I'm a legend."

"Yeah, yeah, me, too," Clint said. "We can still die."

"So I still don't know why you came here to see me," Longarm said. "You got something on your mind?"

"Yeah, I got crazy on my mind," Clint said. "I'm going with you."

"What changed your mind? Billy?"

"I appreciate what it took for you both to ask for help," Clint said. "Also, I read today's paper."

"Ah . . ." Longarm said.

"Yes, ah. I still think you somehow arranged for the waiter to bring me that particular paper."

"How would I have known that you'd want to read a paper?" Longarm asked innocently.

"One way or another," Clint said, "I think that paper would have found its way next to my plate."

"Sorry if it ruined your appetite."

"It didn't," Clint said. "I finished my breakfast. Maybe I didn't taste much of it, but I finished it."

"So two against twenty," Longarm said. "What do you think about those odds?"

Clint hesitated a moment, then said, "Interesting."

"You know," Longarm said, "all we really have to do is bring back Caulfield. The others will scatter without him."

"That's what your marshal said."

"So it's really only two against one," Longarm said. "We've got him outnumbered."

"He's still going to have all those men around him," Clint said.

"Then we'll just have to figure out a way to get him away from them," the deputy said.

"So when do we plan on leaving?" Clint asked.

"First light tomorrow. You can come by the marshal's office and pick up your badge," Longarm said. "Billy did tell you that you'd have to wear a badge, right?"

"We came to an understanding about that."

"You'll have your own horse, and your own guns," Longarm went on, "so all we'll need are some supplies. We'll want to travel light, so we won't be taking any pack horses."

"Suits me."

"Maybe you can locate your friend Slocum and get him to join us," Longarm said.

"I don't know where he is," Clint said, "or I would. I do have a friend in Denver who would be useful, though."

"Oh? Who's that?"

"Talbot Roper."

"The detective," Longarm said. "I know him. He's out of town right now, isn't he?"

"He'll be back at the end of the week. Don't suppose we could wait for him?"

"No," Longarm said, "afraid not. We've got to get on the trail before the gang gets too far away."

"What about a posse?"

"Like I told you before, a bunch of marshals resigned rather than go after them," Longarm said. "You really think we'll be able to get some merchants to leave their stores? Ranchers to leave their ranches and families?"

"No waiters, either."

"How's that?"

"Nothing," Clint said. "I'll meet you in front of the marshal's office, Deputy."

Longarm stuck out his hand.

"I appreciate this, Adams, and the people will, too."

"Yeah, well . . ." Clint said, shaking the man's hand. Nothing came to mind to say.

FOURTEEN

Clint chose not to spend the night with Nancy or Lola, but to get as much rest as he possibly could. He had the feeling that Marshal Long would be a harsh taskmaster on this hunt.

He stopped in the hotel livery and saddled Eclipse, his Darley Arabian.

"I know I told you we'd have some rest, boy," he said, patting the horse's huge neck, "but it seems I have to break my word. It's for a good cause though, or so they tell me."

Eclipse didn't seem too concerned so Clint stopped trying to justify his decision to a horse.

He had checked through his guns the night before, making sure they were all clean and in proper working order. With two against twenty odds, he'd need all the guns he could put his hands on, and he'd have to be confident that they would all work.

All of that done, he mounted Eclipse and rode him to the marshal's office, where he found Deputy Long waiting for him out front.

"You're early," the deputy said.

"Not as early as you."

"It's my job to be early." Longarm was wearing worn

trail clothes today, including a leather vest. He reached into the pocket and held something out to Clint.

"Billy told me about your understanding," he said. "Consider yourself sworn in."

Clint accepted the badge that read *Deputy U.S. Marshal* and put it in his shirt pocket.

"No offense," he said to Longarm.

"None taken."

At that moment, the front door opened and a pasty-faced young man came down the concrete steps to hand Longarm an envelope.

"Your traveling expenses, Deputy," he said. "I know it's futile for me to remind you, but please keep track of your receipts."

"I'll do my best, Henry," Longarm said.

"Please do."

"Don't I always, old son?"

The man rolled his eyes and returned to the building.

"The marshal's clerk," Longarm said to Clint. "We have sort of an understanding, too."

"I can see that."

Longarm tucked the envelope away and mounted his horse. Clint noticed that the horse was outfitted with a Mc-Clellan saddle, which had no saddle horn. He also noticed that the lawman wore a Colt .45 in a cross-draw rig on the left side. Somebody that particular about where he wore his gun was usually pretty good with it.

"You ready, Adams?"

"I'm ready for you to call me Clint, Deputy," Clint said.

"Sorry," Longarm said, "didn't mean any offense."

"None taken, Deputy."

After a moment, Clint figured he was going to continue calling Longarm "Deputy."

"Ready to move out?" Longarm asked.

"Where are we headed?"

"South," Longarm said. "We'll start at the last ranch they burned and track them from there."

"Hope you're a good tracker."

"Decent," Longarm said.

Longarm handed Clint a burlap bag to hang from his saddle. Since they weren't using packhorses they were each carrying a bag with the essentials they'd need to get by on the trail.

They rode in silence until they had left the city limits behind them and then Clint said, "Can you fill me in on Aaron Caulfield?"

"What is there to say?" Longarm asked. "He's a born killer, and he finds it and awakens it in other men. If he chooses a man and can't find it, he kills him."

"Any family?"

"We think he's got cousins riding with him, but no other family, as far as we know."

"Maybe he's looking for brothers."

Longarm looked at Clint.

"Don't overthink this, Ad—Clint. He's a killer, pure and simple, and we're going to put him down."

"And by 'put him down' you mean bring him back to Denver to hang, right?"

"Yeah," Longarm said, "that's right. That's what I mean."

Clint reined his horse in abruptly. Longarm rode several feet, and when he realized Clint had stopped, reined in and turned.

"We need to get something straight," Clint said.

"What's that?"

"There wouldn't be something personal in this for you, would there?" Clint asked. "I mean, Caulfield didn't kill a friend of yours, or a woman, did he?"

"He's killed women and children," Longarm said. "How personal does that have to be for someone to feel outrage?"

"I just have to be sure I'm not backing some kind of personal vendetta here."

"All I'm interested in is upholding the law," Longarm said. "You've got my word on that."

Clint hesitated a moment, then said, "Okay, then."

"Okay," Longarm agreed, and moved out. Clint trotted Eclipse until he caught up to the lawman, and fell into stride with him.

FIFTEEN

Aaron Caulfield sat on the hill and studied the scene below through his field glasses. Behind him his men were broken in to two group. The first was a group of three men, who were all his cousins. Behind them gathered the other twelve, all hired guns.

"He's thinkin' about hittin' another ranch this soon?" Otis Caulfield asked.

His cousin Del Cherry said, "Nobody tells Aaron what to do, Otis."

"I know that," Otis said, "but we're still close to Denver. What if there's a posse out—"

"There's no posse," the third cousin, Leo Caulfield, said. He and Otis were brothers; their mother was sisters with Aaron's mother and Del's.

"How can you be sure?" Del Cherry asked.

"Aaron says so," Leo answered. "He's got it all figured, don't he? Nobody's comin' after us except maybe for one or two marshals who ain't been smart enough to resign."

"Longarm," Otis said.

"What?"

"Longarm," Otis said, again. "He'll come."

"One man, Otis," Leo said. "Why should we be afraid of one man?"

"Because he's Longarm."

"Look at them," Leo said with a jerk of his head.

Otis looked at the other twelve men.

"You think they care if somebody with the crazy name 'Longarm' is comin'?"

"Come on, Leo," Otis said. "There ain't a brain among them. That's why Aaron signed them up. They'll do whatever he says."

"Ain't that what we're supposed to be doin'?" Del Cherry said.

"That's what we are doin'," Leo said. He slapped his brother on the back. "Stop askin' questions, Otis. It ain't exactly healthy."

All three men were properly afraid of their cousin Aaron. Although he was very smart, he was also very crazy. Question him and you might end up looking down the barrel of his gun, a Scholfield he claimed once belonged to Jesse James. He said he bought it from Jesse's wife when he was in St. Jo. His intention was to use Jesse James's own gun to surpass the legend of the man.

"What's he got down there?" Leo asked Del.

"Looks like two women," Cherry said. "Can't tell their ages."

"A man?"

"Yeah."

"Any boys?"

"Can't see any," Del said. "I ain't got the field glass."

They heard movement behind them and turned to see Jerry Stotter approaching. As far as the other eleven men were concerned, Jerry was their ramrod.

"What's goin' on?" he asked. "The men are gettin' restless. Some of 'em say they can smell skirts."

"Two of 'em," Del Cherry said.

"We goin' down?" Stotter asked.

"Guess we got to wait for Aaron to make up his mind," Leo said. "You just tell the men to be patient."

Stotter regarded the three cousins. He didn't like them, that was plain, and all three of them were wary—if not downright afraid—of him. He was a proficient killer, was very good with a gun, and he didn't have to be wooed by Aaron Caulfield. In fact, the cousins thought that Stotter seemed more like a relative of Aaron's than any of them did. They were of the same mind about things.

"Okay," Stotter said. "I'll calm, 'em down."

As he walked back to the other men, Otis said, "Crazy sonofabitch."

"Don't let him hear you say that," Del Cherry said.

"Why do you think I waited for him to walk away?" Otis asked. "I ain't no fool, you know."

"He's standin' up," Leo said. "Must've made up his mind."

The three cousins stood and waited for Aaron Caulfield to reach them and tell them what his decision was.

SIXTEEN

"What's wrong?"

Elizabeth Harrington came up alongside her husband, Ted, who was staring out at apparently nothing, holding his Winchester in his hands.

"Some men on that hill," he said.

"I don't see anyone."

"They're there," he said. "I saw the sun glinting off of glass, probably field glasses."

"What do we do?" she asked.

"Get the girls and go inside," he said. "There are rifles for all of you. You know what windows to man."

They'd only had to do this a time or two, and none of them had ever had to pull the trigger. Elizabeth didn't like the way this felt. They didn't get newspapers out where they lived, but they did hear the news filtering back from Denver. They knew about the men who had been burning ranches, raping women, killing boys and men.

"Ted—"

"Just go inside, Elizabeth," he said. "Nothing may come of this, but I want to be careful."

She nodded, touched his arm, and turned to go back to the house.

"Elizabeth?" he called.

"Yes."

"Make sure your rifle barrels can be seen from the windows."

"All right."

She went into the house with her girls, while Ted Harrington continued to stare up at the hill. He wanted them to know that he knew they were there.

"We're gonna what?" one of the men asked.

"Pass 'em by," Stotter said. He'd gotten the word from the cousins, who'd heard it from Aaron.

"But why?"

"'Cause they got guns down there, and they're waitin'. Words gettin' around. We're gonna have to get farther away from Denver so we can take somebody by surprise."

"Aw hell—" one of the men said, but Jerry Stotter gave him a hard look.

"You want to tell Aaron you disagree?"

The man backed off.

"No."

"I didn't think so," Stotter said. "Mount up. We're movin' out."

When Clint Adams and Custis Long rode up to the Harrington ranch they found Ted standing out in front of the house holding a rifle. The front windows of the house had rifle barrels sticking out. Clint wondered what other windows were being covered.

"Mr. Harrington," Longarm said, "my name is Deputy Marshal Custis Long. This is Clint Adams."

"Did you see them out there?" Harrington asked.

"See who?"

"The men," the rancher said. "They were out there, watching us. I'll bet it was the same men who killed those other families. Burnt them other ranches."

"You might be right about that, Mr. Harrington," Longarm said, "but there are no men out there now. You can put up your rifle . . . and your family can do the same."

"Deputies, you said?" Harrington asked.

"Just like it says on my badge," Longarm said, and leaned closer to give the rancher a good look.

"Well," Ted Harrington said, reluctantly lowering his rifle, "all right. If you say so."

"I says so, sir," Longarm said.

"Well . . . you best come inside, then. Elizabeth can rustle up some grub."

"You got boys who can tend to our horses?" Longarm asked.

"I got daughters, but they can tend your horses. You fellas step down and come eat."

While the Harrington girls—looking all of twelve and fourteen—cared for their horses, Clint and Longarm sat at the Harrington table, while Elizabeth Harrington prepared a meal. Ted told them about the three-day vigil he and his family had just been through.

"You say they were here three days ago?" Longarm asked.

"Up on that rise east of the ranch," Harrington said.

"Did your wife . . . ma'am, did you see them, as well?"

Elizabeth looked to her husband for the answer but he said, "Tell the truth, Beth."

"I did not see them," she said, "but if my husband says he saw them, then they were there."

"We believe him, Mrs. Harrington," Clint said. "We're just trying to come up with more information on these critters we're tracking."

"Critters?" she asked.

"Clint and I are pretty much of a like mind about them, ma'am," Longarm said. "They're not men, they're animals."

The two girls came into the house, smiling shyly.

"Just in time for supper, girls," their mother said. "Help me set the table."

Clint and Longarm ate with the family, and then while the mother and daughters saw to cleaning the kitchen, the men went out on the front porch. Ted Harrington accepted Longarm's offer of a cigar and both men lit up. Clint declined.

"All right, Ted," Longarm said, "now that we're out of earshot of the women, suppose you tell us what you saw?"

"I didn't actually see anyone, if that's what you mean," Harrington said. "It was more like . . . a feeling, you know? When you can tell you're being watched?"

Clint and Longarm both nodded. They had each experienced that themselves.

"And then there was this glint of light," Harrington went on. "A reflection, really, like somebody was using a set of field glasses to watch us."

"Where did you see it?"

"Up on that hill," Harrington said, pointing. It was dark, but they knew what hill he was referring to.

"Seems to me you got lucky, Ted," Clint said. "Must've been those gun barrels sticking out your windows that put them off. They must've gone looking for an easier target."

"My wife and my girls can shoot," Harrington said. "Without sons, I had to make them learn."

"It was a good idea," Longarm said. "We'll bunk in the barn, if you don't mind."

"Make yourselves comfortable."

"We'll head out at first light," Longarm said, "check out that hill first, see if we can find anything helpful."

"I think you can probably relax, Ted," Clint said. "Stop keeping guard all the time. I think they moved on."

"I hope you're right," Harrington said, "but I think I'll just be vigilant another couple of days, just to make sure."

"Can't blame you for that," Longarm said.

"We'll say good night to your wife," Clint said, "and then join our horses in the barn."

• • •

After they had each set up a hay bed for themselves they removed their hats and gun belts and tried to get comfortable.

"Would've been a real shame if we'd gotten here and found that family slaughtered," Clint said.

"Beautiful family," Longarm said. "They escaped, but there's another beautiful family out there somewhere that won't, unless we stop Caulfield and his men."

"Well," Clint said, "that's what we're out here to do."

And for the first time since he'd agreed to accompany Longarm on his hunt, Clint truly felt it was his duty, too.

SEVENTEEN

They rose together the next morning, washed in a horse trough, donned their hats and guns, and saddled their horses. The Harrington family was awake and waved at them as they rode their horses up to the top of the hill Harrington had told them about.

When they reached the top they dismounted and walked around a bit.

"I see prints from a dozen horses, maybe more," Clint said.

"Not only that," Longarm said. "Look here. They split into groups. Most of them here, then over here maybe three different animals." He walked a bit farther, then said, "And here. One more."

He got down to one knee, held his hands to his eyes as if he were holding a pair of field glasses.

"This was Caulfield," he said. "This was where he watched them from."

Clint walked over and stood behind Longarm. From his vantage point he could see the Harrington ranch clearly.

"Why would they be afraid of a few guns?" he wondered aloud.

Longarm stood up.

"The Harringtons were showing just enough resistance," the lawman said. "Also, I think we're too close to Denver. Caulfield probably wants to put some distance between him and his last slaughter before he tries again."

"If that's the case," Clint said, "if it wasn't the presence of the extra guns that put him off, then that family down there simply lucked out."

"Their good fortune is going to be somebody else's bad," Longarm predicted.

Longarm took extra time looking over the tracks that had been made by Caulfield and his horse. Clint knew Longarm was memorizing what the man's boot prints looked like, and his horse's hoofprints. This, to Clint's mind, made Longarm an excellent tracker.

The two men mounted up again.

"Tracks head south," Longarm said.

"Then that's where we're headed."

They rode in silence for a few moments and then Longarm said, "Why do I feel you're suddenly more committed to this?"

"Because you're observant," Clint said. "I just think about Harrington's family—beautiful wife, lovely daughters—and how we might have come across them . . ."

"I know," Longarm said. "I thought about that, too, last night, trying to sleep."

"So, yeah," Clint said, "I'm committed."

"Committed enough to pin that badge on where folks can see it?"

"Let's not get carried away."

Clint and Longarm continued to follow the tracks left by the gang, but came across no further acts of violence by them in Colorado.

The tracks began to drift in a westerly fashion, to the point where Clint and Longarm started to wonder if Caulfield was taking his men to New Mexico, or to Arizona.

"And if they keep going west," Longarm said over their campfire later that evening "they may end up taking us to Utah."

"How far can we track them?"

"We've got Billy Vail's leave to follow them to hell if we have to," Longarm replied.

"That's what I was hoping you'd say."

They were camped outside of Durango. They figured the gang still had the choice of riding either to New Mexico or Arizona or heading due west for Utah. By mid-afternoon the next day the tracks would probably paint a much clearer picture for them.

Or so they thought.

"What's he doin'?" one of the men asked Stotter.

"Switching horses."

"But . . . why? He's got a good animal."

"It's how he stays careful," Stotter said. "Nobody tracking us will be able to figure out which horse he's ridin' if he keeps switching."

"I wondered," the other man said. He'd seen Caulfield do it before—usually switching horses with one of his cousins—but he'd never asked why before now.

Aaron Caulfield's three cousins didn't like it when he switched horses with them. For one thing, Leo and Otis both liked their horses. As for Dell Cherry, he just didn't like the idea that some tracker might mistake him for his more notorious cousin.

Today, Aaron had forced Otis to exchange animals with him, saddle and all.

"Aaron," Otis complained, "why don't you switch with Stotter for a change?"

"Jerry likes his horse."

"I like my horse."

Aaron gave Otis a hard look.

"He ain't my cousin. He ain't blood."

That kept Otis from asking why Aaron didn't switch with one of the other men.

Aaron walked away from the others with his new animal. When they camped, he always kept to himself, preferring his own campfire. The three cousins did the same. The other men sometimes built one or two, depending on how much wood was around.

The cousins hunkered down around their campfire and poured some harsh trail coffee. Other than that, all they had was some beef jerky.

"We've got to hit a town soon," Otis said. "We need some supplies."

"We don't even know where he's takin' us," Leo said. "What if he wants to go to Utah Territory? I don't wanna go to Utah."

"None of us wanna go there," Del said. "I don't think that's what he's plannin'."

"Then what?" Leo asked.

"Go ask 'im," Del Cherry said. "What are you afraid of? He's your cousin."

"He's your cousin, too."

"I ain't the one with questions."

Leo looked at his brother for help.

"Don't look at me," Otis said. "I ain't askin' him. He took my horse."

"You'll get it back," Del said. "You know he switches every few days."

"I know it," Otis said, "but I ain't gotta like it."

"Hey," Leo said suddenly. "Where's he goin'?"

They all looked up and saw Jerry Stotter walking over to where Aaron Caulfield was sitting.

EIGHTEEN

Aaron looked up as Stotter approached.

"Jerry."

"Aaron."

"The men got a complaint?"

"No complaints," Stotter said. "We was just wonderin' where we're headed, is all."

Aaron turned and looked at his three cousins.

"They're wonderin', too, but they ain't got the balls to ask." He shook his head. "How'd I end up with them as family?"

"Ya don't get to pick your family, I guess," Stotter said. "Del's okay, though."

"Yeah, maybe," Aaron said, turning back around, "but the other two are idiots. So was their mother. My pa says she hit her head on the bedpost once too often."

"Everything okay with you, Aaron?"

"Yeah, why wouldn't it be?"

"The boys were just wonderin' . . ."

Aaron stared up at Stotter.

"There's another cup there," he said. "Pour yourself some coffee and hunker down. You're makin' my neck hurt."

"Thanks."

Stotter did as he was told and sat down on the other side of the fire.

"The boys're gettin' anxious, huh?"

"They want some action."

"They'll get some," Caulfield said. "The next place we hit is gonna be big. Women, money, horses, we're gonna get everythin' we want. Don't worry."

"I ain't worried, Aaron," Stotter said. "I just do what I'm told."

"Yeah, now you do," Aaron said.

They drank in silence a few moments, then Caulfield said, "I'm thinkin' of makin' some cuts."

"Cuts?"

"Yeah. We're too easy to track this way," Aaron said. "Too big a group. I never meant for us to get this big."

"Who you gonna cut?"

"I don't know," Aaron said, "but it won't be you, or my idiot cousins." He paused a moment. "I may kill them, but I won't cut them."

"I'll kill 'em for ya," Stotter said. "Just say the word."

Aaron Caulfield froze, then asked, "Is that supposed to be funny?"

"Huh? Oh, yeah, well, it was—"

"They're family, Jerry," Aaron said.

"I'm sorry, I didn't mean—"

"If anybody's gonna kill 'em it'll be me," Aaron said. "You got that?"

Stotter didn't know if Aaron was kidding or not so he just said, "I got it. I better get back to the men."

He tossed the remnants of his coffee into the fire, set the cup aside, and stood up.

"Don't say anything to them about what we talked about," Aaron said. "That's just between you and me."

"Gotcha."

"Okay."

Stotter turned and walked back to where the men were camped. As he passed the cousins he could sense that they were all watching him. He knew they were dying to know what he and Aaron had talked about. He deliberately did not look their way.

"What do you suppose that was about?" Otis asked.

"I don't know," Leo said, "but I'd like to."

"So go ask 'im," Del Cherry said. "He's your cousin."

"He's your cousin, too," Otis said.

"Don't start that again," Del said. "I told you, I ain't that interested."

"Leo?"

"Me, neither," Leo said. "You wanna know, go ask him."

Instead, Otis mumbled to himself and reached for the coffeepot.

Aaron Caulfield watched Jerry Stotter return to his place among the other men, then looked over at his cousins— two idiots and one near idiot. Stotter was right—Del Cherry was okay, but he had to be told what to do. There was no initiative there.

Aaron could feel the impatience of the other men in the air. He shared it with them. What they didn't know was that, to him, it was not only impatience, but it was also a need.

He put his hand on his gun and caressed it. He didn't know why he was only happy when he was watching the light of life go out in the eyes of another, but that was the case. And if there was fear there at the same time, even better.

Though he thrived on death, Aaron Caulfield was no animal. He did not kill indiscriminately. He killed when the need arose in him, and he did not try to justify it. He broke the laws of man and God with equal impunity, and didn't care that he would eventually have to pay for it. After all, what man was not going to die, eventually?

He simply intended to send as many people to their maker as he could before he went himself.

NINETEEN

Clint made coffee and breakfast the next morning. They were in no hurry and could afford to start with a meal. The trail was clear enough, and if the gang was going to hit another ranch this soon they had probably done it already. There was already a sense of urgency. What they did not need was a sense of panic, or desperation, in their hunt.

"Thanks," Longarm said, as Clint handed him a cup of coffee and a plate of eggs. "I tell you yet you make a helluva pot of trail coffee?"

"My specialty," Clint said. "I like a good pot of strong coffee when I'm in town, or in a city like Denver or New York, but this is what I need to keep me going on the trail."

"I think we need to discuss something we didn't discuss in Denver," the lawman said.

"What's that?"

"Who's in charge," Longarm said.

"You mean, who's the boss here?" Clint asked.

"What I mean is, who'll make the decisions when we catch up to them."

"I assumed we'd discuss it."

"You assume we're on equal footing here?"

"Yes."

"Why's that?"

"Because I'm not really a deputy," Clint said. "I don't actually have any official standing. And I figure I'm along to help you, and to keep you alive."

Longarm scratched his chin.

"Is that a fact?"

"I don't know if it's a fact, Deputy," Clint said, "but it's how I see it. Now why don't you tell me how you see it?"

"Okay. This is my job, and I take it very seriously. I'm good at it, but I'm used to making my own decisions."

"Are you used to giving orders?" Clint asked.

"Not usually," Longarm said, "but then I usually work alone."

"So this is an unusual situation, right?"

"Agreed."

"I'll tell you what," Clint said. "I'll concede to you whenever we're in a situation where you have more experience."

"That sounds fair."

"And I'll expect the same courtesy."

"Of course."

What each man didn't know was that the other was only agreeing because he did not ever expect to be in that situation. Each felt he had significant enough experience that the other would never supersede him. In Clint's mind the only thing Longarm had more experience in was actually wearing a badge.

Which really didn't amount to much.

Aaron Caulfield woke that morning with a decision already made. It surprised him, and it surprised everyone else, too.

"You want us to what?" Otis asked.

"I want you to take half the men and continue south," Aaron said.

"And what are you gonna do?" Leo asked.

"Take the other half and go west."

"Why?"

"Because I say so."

Otis and Leo exchanged looks.

"Which men?" Leo asked.

"You choose," Aaron said. "Del and Stotter are comin' with me, but other than that, you pick."

"How many?" Otis asked.

"Half," Aaron said, then, "six. Counting you two, that would be eight."

"And what are we supposed to do?" Leo asked.

"Do what we do, Leo," Aaron said.

"You mean . . . make a score? Pick one out, go ahead and do it without you?" Leo asked.

"That's right, Leo," Aaron said. "That's what I want you to do."

"But wh—"

Aaron raised an index finger and said, "Don't ask why. Just do it. Jerry?"

Stotter, who along with the cousins had been summoned to Aaron's fire, had been listening.

"Yep?"

"Tell the men what's gonna happen."

"Okay."

"Make sure they know they have to listen to Otis and Leo."

"Okay."

"Go on," he said to his cousins. "Go with Jerry."

The two brothers again exchanged confused glances, but followed Stotter.

"What are you doin', Aaron?" Del Cherry asked.

"I'm cuttin' the herd, Del," Aaron said. "We got too many men."

"Yeah, but . . . Leo and Otis? They're family."

"You wanna go with them?"

"No, but—"

"This will tell me if they've got half a brain between them," Aaron said. "If they don't, then I don't want them around. You got it?"

"I got it, Aaron."

"Then get saddled," Aaron said. "We're headin' west."

TWENTY

When Clint and Longarm reached the cold campsite they dismounted and walked around it.

"Same as the others," Longarm said. "He keeps himself apart from the rest."

"Not the same at all," Clint said, pointing.

Longarm came over to have a look for himself and saw what Clint was talking about.

"They've split."

"Yup."

"Half went south, the other half west."

"What do you want?" Clint asked. "New Mexico or Utah?"

Longarm didn't answer. He went to take a closer look at the prints left by all the horses.

"So?" Clint asked. "Should we split or follow one group?"

"You're asking me?"

"It's your job—as you told me."

Longarm pointed to the ground.

"That's his horse," Longarm said. "He's gone south. We should go that way."

"What if that's not him?"

"What?"

"I'm just saying," Clint replied. "What if he switched horses with someone?"

"Why would he do that?"

"In case he's being followed."

"There's no way he knows we're trailing him," Longarm said.

"You mean there's no way he can know it's us," Clint said. "But he's got to figure somebody's coming after him."

Longarm looked annoyed.

"Look, when you're a lawman you have to stick to the facts," he told Clint.

"We don't have any facts, Deputy," Clint said. "We're out here pissing into the wind. What if this isn't even Caulfield and his gang we're following?"

"That's crazy," Longarm said dismissively.

"I'm just throwing possibilities out there."

"How can we make decisions based on possibilities?" the lawman asked.

The two men had bickered quietly ever since leaving Denver. They had argued over who would make camp, who should break camp, who should see to the horses. Clint knew that even though they had discussed who was in charge and agreed to consult each other, the badge Longarm wore made him feel he had the right to dictate their actions.

Longarm knew that Clint Adams's reputation would make it hard for him to take orders, so he tried to subtly make their decisions, hoping Clint would not notice.

"I'll tell you what," Clint said. "You follow that group." He pointed south. "I'll follow this one. We're closing in on them. Eventually, we'll catch up and be able to tell which group he's with."

"We only have a description of him," Longarm said. "You won't know him on sight."

Clint took a deep breath.

"But his campfire will be separate from the others," Clint said. "It'll be obvious."

Longarm took a moment to think.

"All right," he said finally. "But as soon as you catch up and see he's not with them you'll have to catch up to me. I'm not going to try to take him alone."

"And neither am I," Clint said. "I'm not looking forward to facing six or eight men by myself."

Longarm hesitated.

"I still don't know if this is a good idea."

"Look, the longer we wait the less chance there is that it is a good idea," Clint said. He knew they could stand there and discuss the thing to death. "Let's just get moving."

They mounted up.

"Just don't get yourself killed trying something foolish," Longarm told him.

"I'm not looking to get myself killed trying to bring this man in," Clint said. "That's something we're going to do together."

Longarm stared at Clint, who, realizing how that had come out, said, "You know what I mean."

They didn't bother divvying up the supplies, just kept whatever they were carrying. They were hoping to be able to meet up again before the need for more supplies arose.

"Personally," Clint said, "I hope they went to New Mexico or Arizona."

"Why?"

Clint shrugged.

"I just like them better. Who wants to go to Utah?"

"Well, I don't care where I catch him," Longarm said, "just as long as I catch him."

"We'll catch him."

The two men shook hands.

"See you soon," Clint said.

"Ride careful, old son," Longarm said.

TWENTY-ONE

Away from Longarm for the first time in days, Clint felt as if he could breathe again. The weight of their two reputations, not to mention their two egos, had pressed heavily on both of them. Clint knew he probably should have been the bigger man, given in, and allowed the deputy to be in charge. It was just that the man's attitude irked him.

Splitting up probably had not been the smartest decision. After all, he was supposed to be along to make sure the lawman didn't get killed. But if splitting up could help them eliminate half the men, it would make grabbing Aaron Caulfield that much easier—not that it was going to be an easy task at all.

Clint knew that a single man on a horse moved faster than a group of men together. That was just the way it was. There was something about a large group that just kept them moving slower than they would have individually. For this reason, as the hours went by, the tracks he was following became fresher and fresher.

Finally, he came to a signpost announcing that the town of Liberty was ahead two miles. From the tracks, that looked to be where the men were heading as well.

The badge in his pocket felt heavy, but not as heavy as it would have been pinned to his chest, like a huge bulls-eye.

He directed Eclipse down the road toward Liberty.

Otis and Leo rode ahead of the other six men so they could talk freely without being heard.

"It's been hours," Leo said to Otis. "What do we do?"

"Whataya mean, 'what do we do?' " Leo asked. "We do what Aaron told us to do."

They rode in silence for a few moments and then Otis asked, "What did he tell us to do?"

"Pull a job," Leo said. "He told us to find a job and do it."

"We ain't never picked one out before," Otis said. "How do we do that?"

"We watched Aaron plenty of times, Otis," Leo said. "We just gotta find a ranch that looks rich and take it."

"A rich ranch will have ranch hands," Otis said. "How do we find one that ain't?"

"I don't know," Leo said, "but he always does, so we gotta—and don't talk so damn loud. We don't want the others to think we don't know what we're doin'."

"But Leo."

"What?"

"We don't."

"Shut up."

As Longarm followed the tracks, he saw that they were becoming fresher. If he was catching up to his quarry, then Clint Adams had to be doing the same.

Adams, he thought, what can ego! Just couldn't take orders, could he? He hoped the man's gun was worth keeping him around.

"I got it," Otis said.

"Got what?" Leo asked.

"A job."

"Otis," his brother said, "you ain't supposed to be tryin' to think of a job."

"I know," Otis said, "but one came to me, just the same."

Since Leo didn't have any ideas he said, "Okay then, what?"

"A bank."

"You mean . . . rob a bank?"

"Why not?" Otis asked. "It's better than a ranch."

"We ain't never robbed a bank, Otis."

"I'll bet some of them have," Otis said, motioning toward the other men.

"Oh, great, so we're gonna ask *them* how to do it?" Leo asked. "We can't be in charge if we do that."

"You can figure out a way, Leo," Otis said. "You're the smart one."

"I am?"

"Smarter than me, anyway."

Behind them the six men rode, wondering what they had done to deserve this. Why had Aaron Caulfield placed them in the hands of his two idiot cousins?

"We can't do this," Ed Lando said. "We can't follow these two."

"What do you suggest?" his partner, Joe Rabe, asked.

They were riding drag, lagging behind the rest.

"Let's get out of here, Joe," Lando said. "Aaron's obviously cut us loose. Let's go out on our own."

"What about the others?" Rabe asked, indicating the riders ahead of them.

"What do we care?" Lando asked.

"I don't know . . ."

"You got a better idea?" Lando asked.

"I think we should wait, Ed."

"For what?"

"Just a little bit longer," Rabe said, "to see if Aaron has some kind of plan."

"Yeah, he has a plan," Lando said. "To get rid of us."

"Why us?" Rabe asked. "Why would he do that?"

"Maybe you can ask him, next time we see him."

Rabe looked over at his compadre riding alongside him.

"Just a little longer, Ed. Okay?"

Lando sighed.

"Okay, Joe," he said. "Just a little longer."

TWENTY-TWO

When Clint rode into the town of Liberty he had no idea what he'd find. The tracks he'd been following had dispersed just outside of town. It was as if all of the men and horses had split up, some going around the town, some riding into it.

Longarm had been pretty sure Aaron Caulfield had ridden into New Mexico. Clint wondered if he should abandon his course at this point and catch up to the deputy.

He decided to have a look around before making that decision. He didn't have long to wait.

Liberty was a small town, with not much activity going on. He spotted two horses in front of the General Store, and could tell by their condition that they had been ridden hard recently. It made sense for most of the men to wait outside, while perhaps two—like these two—rode into town for supplies.

Clint reined Eclipse in about a block away from the General Store and loosely strung his reins over the hitching post. He stepped up onto the boardwalk and started toward the store. He wondered if this town had any law to speak of, but he didn't have time to go looking.

As he approached the General Store two men came out

carrying packages wrapped in brown paper. They both wore guns, and had their hands full.

They started to step down to their horses when Clint called out, "Hold it right there."

Both men stopped short and stiffened.

"Turn this way."

Both men obeyed and looked surprised when they saw him.

"Whataya want, mister?" one of them demanded.

"We ain't done nothin'," the other said.

"Guess that remains to be seen," Clint said. "These horses look pretty hard ridden. Where did you come from? And where are you headed?"

"You ain't the law," one said.

"Yeah, I don't see no badge," the second tossed in. "We ain't gotta say nothin' to you."

"That's where you're wrong."

Clint had two choices: draw his gun or show the badge Longarm had given him. He decided on the badge, only because he didn't like to draw his gun unless he was going to use it.

He took the badge from his pocket and showed it to the two men.

"Does that help?" he asked.

"Why don't ya wear it?" one man asked.

"It makes holes in my shirt," Clint said.

"We gotta put these supplies down, mister," one said. "Our arms are gettin' real tired."

"That's okay," Clint said, "stay that way a little longer."

"What's this all about, mister?" the other one asked. He was tall and blond, about thirty. The other was older, near forty, and squat. Clint wondered how they had been chosen to come in for the supplies.

"I'm going to ask you one question," Clint said. "If you answer it, then we won't have any trouble."

"What?" the older one asked.

"Aaron Caulfield," Clint said. "Is he with you, or did he ride with the other group?"

The two men hesitated, then one asked, "Aaron who?"

And the other, "What group?"

"Those aren't the right answers," Clint said. "I think I'm going to let you men put down those supplies."

"You gonna kill us?" the young one asked.

"We ain't done nothin' to you," the other said.

"I'm not going to kill you," Clint said. "I'm going to let you put those supplies down . . . in the sheriff's office."

The two men exchanged nervous looks with each other. They didn't want to go to the sheriff's office. There must have been papers out on both of them.

"Hey, mister," the older one said, "give us a break, huh? We don't know what yer talkin' about, but we don't wanna go to the sheriff's office."

"We don't get along with the law," the young one said.

"Well, you're either going to have to talk to me, or the local law," Clint said. "Take your pick."

"Don't much like either choice," the young one said.

"I think we might have to take our chances with you," the older one said. "It's two against one."

"But your hands are full."

"You'd let us put this stuff down, right?" the older one asked. "To make for a fair fight?"

"Fair fight?" Clint asked. "Is that what you call two against one? I think what you're going to have to do is drop those supplies and go for your guns. If one of you survives, he'll talk to me."

The two men remained silent.

"I wonder which of you will live, though?" Clint said.

"It ain't gonna be you," the older one said. "We can take 'im, Billy Boy."

"What's your name, mister?" the young one asked. "I don't like to kill a man if I don't know his name."

"My name's Clint Adams, Billy Boy," Clint said. "Been

following you boys since Denver. You got a lot to answer for."

But they weren't really listening to what he was saying, not since they heard his name.

"Adams?" the older one asked.

"Clint Adams?" Billy Boy asked.

"That's right."

They exchanged nervous glances again, each licking his lips.

"Well," Clint said, "let's get to it, then. You better commence to dropping those supplies and going for your guns. I don't have all day, you know."

Learning his name would either keep them from going for their guns, or spook them into drawing. Whichever it was, he could wait.

TWENTY-THREE

Outside of Liberty, Aaron Caulfield waited with Del Cherry, Jerry Stotter, and the other men. He was convinced he had done the right thing, not by sending Billy Boy and Dugan into town, but by sending Leo and Otis and the others away—although Rabe and Lando were pretty good boys. He had an idea that those two would get along on their own, though.

"Takin' too long," Stotter said.

"Are we close enough to town to hear shots?" Del asked.

"I don't know."

"Take it easy," Aaron told both of them. "If they're not back in half an hour we'll move on."

"Leave more men behind?" Stotter asked.

Aaron looked over at the remaining three men.

"These are pretty good men," he said. "I think the six of us would make a great gang, don't you boys?"

"Well . . . sure, Aaron," Del Cherry said. "But what about Leo and Otis? I mean, if they come back."

"Forget about Leo and Otis," Aaron said. "You saw what they were like at that last ranch. They became liabilities, Del."

95

"Well, okay," Del said, "they went a little wild, but they learned it from—"

"You gonna be a liability too, Del?" Aaron asked.

Cherry looked at his cousin, and at Jerry Stotter. As far as Del was concerned, Aaron was the meanest man he knew, and Stotter was the fastest with a gun.

"No, Aaron," he said. "No, I ain't."

"Twenty-five minutes," Aaron said, "and then we're movin' out. We'll get supplies somewhere else—maybe the next ranch we come to."

"Fuck it," Dugan said. He opened his arms, let the bags drop to the ground, and went for his gun. He was too slow. Clint was so fast his first bullet went through one of the packages before it ripped into Dugan's belly.

Billy Boy was even slower; he never cleared leather as Clint covered him.

"Wait, wait!" Billy raised his hands, letting his packages crash to the ground. "Don't kill me!"

"We'll be getting some company soon, Billy Boy," Clint said. "Towns people are already coming this way. Shouldn't be too long before the sheriff gets here."

"Don't kill me," Billy begged, "but don't gimme to no sheriff, neither."

"Tell me about Aaron Caulfield, Billy," Clint said. "Which group is he with?"

Billy hesitated, licked his lips.

"Which one, Billy?" Clint said. "I'm not going to ask again."

"Shots," Stotter said.

"I didn't hear nothin'," Del Cherry said.

"If Jerry says he heard shots, he heard shots," Aaron said to his cousin. "Get the men mounted. We're movin' out."

"Want me to go back?" Stotter asked Aaron as Del Cherry went to rouse the other men.

"No," Aaron said. "Just mount up. If those two found trouble we don't want it findin' us, too."

"Okay, Aaron," Stotter said. "You're the boss."

As Stotter mounted, Aaron looked around at the remainder of his gang. Good size, he thought. The other way there'd been just too damn many, especially when they went wild like Otis and Leo had. He just couldn't control them.

Although, he was thinking now, maybe he should have just killed them.

"He's waitin' outside of town," Billy Boy told Clint. "Aaron Caulfield and more men."

"So he didn't ride with the group that went south."

"No."

"But his horse . . ."

"He changes horses," Billy said. "It's somethin' he does every few days."

Longarm wasn't going to like it much that Clint had been right about the horse.

"How many men with him?" Clint asked.

"Five," Billy said, "six countin' him."

"You got any idea why he split the gang up?"

"No," the younger man said. "We was wonderin'."

At that moment a man wearing a badge stepped through a group of men who had gathered to watch.

"What's goin' on here?" the man demanded.

Clint took out the deputy marshal's badge and showed it to him.

"Got a man for your jail, Sheriff," Clint said, "but I don't have a lot of time to explain why, so listen up."

"Hey," Billy Boy protested, "you said you wasn't gonna turn me over to the law if I talked."

"Did I say that?" Clint asked. "I don't remember that, Billy. Not at all."

TWENTY-FOUR

Otis and Leo had decided there was no way around it—they had to approach the other men about robbing a bank. It was all they could think of, until they came within sight of the ranch house.

"You see what I see?" Otis asked.

"I see it."

The house was a wooden two-story structure, with a corral and barn next to it. There didn't appear to be many hands there.

"Either they're out workin'," Leo said, "or there just ain't any."

"Look like money to you, Leo?" Otis asked.

"If there ain't," Leo said, "it'll be good practice for us."

"I see a clothesline, too," Otis said. "I see dresses."

Ed Lando and Joe Rabe decided to be insulted. They also decided that the other men could fend for themselves. They were going to head back north, try to catch up with Aaron and the other men.

"I ain't afraid of Aaron," Rabe said. "He better have a good explanation for what he's done."

"You ain't afraid of him?" Lando asked.

"No."

"Then why didn't you ask him in the first place?"

"I . . . didn't think of it," Rabe muttered.

They were about to make their move when they noticed some commotion up ahead.

"What's goin' on?" Lando said aloud.

"Let's go and find out," Rabe suggested.

It was a matter of hours before Longarm came within sight of the other eight men. He also saw, beyond them, the ranch house. He had no way of knowing if Aaron Caulfield was among them, but that really wouldn't have changed anything. He had to do something to keep them from hitting that house.

The eight men—some mounted, some dismounted—seemed to be having a palaver about it. Maybe Caulfield wasn't with them. If he was he'd be telling them what to do, and there wouldn't be any discussion.

Longarm thought he had time to circle them and make it down to the house before they made their move. He decided to circle to the left, where there was some cover, and keep an eye on them. If they made a move toward the house he'd have no choice but to start shooting. Maybe he'd even be able to lure them away. But if he got to the house first he'd be able to warn the occupants. Maybe there'd be enough guns there to fight the gang off.

He stopped thinking about it and started his move.

"You two are idiots," Joe Rabe said. He looked around at the other men. "Any objections to that?"

The other men shook their heads.

"We ain't no idiots," Otis said, "we just ain't that smart."

"But we're Aaron's blood," Leo pointed out.

"Fat lot of good that done you," Lando said. "He got rid of you like he did us."

"Got rid of us?" Otis asked.

"Why do you think he sent us this way?" Rabe asked. "He decided to thin the herd, and we was all chuff."

"We're on our own," Lando said, looking down at the house. "This don't look like a prime job, but it's all we got." He and Rabe didn't bother telling the others they were going to leave afterward. And if they could leave with most of the take from this job, even better.

"So what are we gonna do?" one of the other men asked.

"We're goin' down hard and fast," Joe Rabe said. "Take what we want, torch the house."

"What about the women?" Otis asked, his eyes shining. "I see dresses hanging outside."

"You do what you want with the women," Rabe said. "We want money, or goods."

"What the hell is that?" Lando asked suddenly.

They all looked down at the house and saw a rider approaching it fast.

"Who is that?" Rabe demanded.

"Anybody got glasses?" Lando asked, but no one but Aaron had a set of field glasses.

"What do we do?" Leo asked. "We don't know who he is."

"It don't matter who he is," Rabe said. "He's one man. We do this all the time."

"Yeah," one of the others said, "but with more men."

"You don't think we can do this with eight?" Ed Lando demanded. "Then you go ahead and leave. We'll do it with seven. And we'll keep your share of the goods."

"I ain't leavin'," the man said. "I was just sayin'."

"Well, stop sayin'," Joe Rabe said, gathering up his reins, "and let's start doin'."

TWENTY-FIVE

Clint convinced the sheriff to take the prisoner while he rode out to see if he could catch up to Caulfield and the rest of his men. He did reach the place where they had obviously been waiting for their supplies, but they were gone. He wanted to continue to track them, but knew he had to go back to Liberty and talk to the local law. He couldn't just kill a man and ride away.

"Thought I might have to come lookin' for you," the sheriff said when Clint walked into his office.

"I told you I'd be back."

"Coffee?" the lawman asked.

Clint sat down in a chair in front of the man's desk and said, "Yeah, sounds good."

The sheriff poured two cups, handed Clint one, and sat behind his desk.

"Name's Anderson, Ted Anderson. Been sheriff around here for a dozen years or so."

"Clint Adams."

Anderson's eyebrows went up.

"I didn't hear nothin' about you wearin' a badge now."

"As you can see," Clint said, "I'm not. I'm carrying it in my pocket."

"Been sworn in?"

"Kind of. I'm really just helping out a fellow named Custis Long."

"The one they call Longarm?"

"That's right."

"Longarm and the Gunsmith workin' together."

"Not very well, I'm afraid."

"Where is he?"

"We split up when this gang did," Clint said. "I think he's in New Mexico somewhere."

"What gang is this supposed to be?"

"You heard of Aaron Caulfield?"

The lawman thought a minute, then shook his bald head.

"Can't say I have."

"They've been killing some people around Denver," Clint said. "Now they're on the move and we're tracking them."

"And these two were part of that gang?"

"That's right."

"How many others you trackin'?"

"I guess we're trailing about eight each."

"Eight each?"

"That's right."

"Leaves six for you." His tone made it clear he didn't think either of them was very smart for tracking that many men alone. "Which group has the boss in it?"

"That's what I was trying to find out," Clint said. "It's why I tried to leave one of them alive."

"Guess you wanna talk to him, then. Key's on a peg on the wall just inside the door. Help yourself."

"Thanks." Clint put the coffee on the desk and walked into the cell block. He ignored the key and walked to the cell the young man was in.

"How're you doing, Billy Boy?"

The man didn't answer. He was sitting on a bunk, staring down at the floor.

"Is that really your name or just what they call you?"

"What's the difference?"

"Listen," Clint said. "I need you to answer a couple of questions. If you do, it might go easier on you."

Suddenly, the young man looked interested. He looked up from the floor.

"What kinda questions?"

"Well, just two, really."

"All I gotta do is answer two questions?"

"That's right."

"And you'll let me go?"

"I didn't say that," Clint replied. "I said things might go easier for you."

Billy Boy thought that over, then said, "What are the questions?"

"Were you telling me the truth when you told me Caulfield was riding with your group and waiting outside town?"

Billy thought that over a minute, then apparently decided there was no harm in answering.

"Yes."

"Good," Clint said. "Now the second question: where is he headed?"

"That I don't know," Billy said. "He don't tell us his plans. And he only talks to his cousins, and to Jerry Stotter."

"Stotter? He's riding with Caulfield?"

"That's right," Billy said, and then, "Hey, that was a third question."

But Clint was already leaving the cell block.

"Get anything out of him?" the sheriff asked.

"What I wanted and more," Clint said. "Apparently, I'm tracking the right group. Caulfield is definitely with them."

"That's good, right?"

"Depends on how you look at it. He's got Jerry Stotter with him."

"Stotter? Jesus, he's a pretty fast gun."

"That's what I've heard."

"In fact, some say he might even be as fast as you."

Clint looked at the man and said, "Yeah, I've heard that, too."

TWENTY-SIX

Clint decided there was no rush to ride into a group of guns that included Jerry Stotter—not alone, anyway. It would be dusk soon, and the trail would be clear enough come morning. He decided to get a hotel room, a drink, and a steak, in that order.

While he was having the steak, the sheriff walked into the restaurant and came over to his table.

"Have a seat, Sheriff," he said. "Join me for a steak?"

"Had one," the man said, sitting anyway. "They brought me one and one to your boy in the cell."

"What's on your mind, then?"

"You still goin' after that gang?"

"My part of them, anyway," Clint said. "First light I'll be moving out. You thinking of coming with me?"

"Oh, no," the man said, "not me. This sounds like a lot of time in the saddle and my ass can't take that anymore."

"Got any deputies you could send with me?"

"Not a one."

"They won't go with me?"

"Ain't got any deputies," the man said. "Nobody hereabouts wants the job. And to tell you the truth, this town

107

don't really need 'em. Except for your shootin' today we ain't seen any trouble in a long time."

"Well, that's good for you and the town," Clint said. "Bad for me."

"What about Longarm?" the sheriff asked. "Think he'll catch up to you?"

"Don't know that I can count on that," Clint said. "Of course, if he shows up you can point him in the right direction. I'd be obliged."

"Be happy to. Pointin' is somethin' I can still do without damaging my ass." He pushed his chair back and stood up. "I'll let you finish your steak. Stop by my office in the morning before you leave."

"You'll be there that early?"

"Like I said," Anderson replied, "I got no deputies and now, thanks to you, I got a prisoner."

"I'll drop by."

The sheriff left, passing the waiter, who was bringing over another pot of coffee.

Aaron Caulfield called both Del Cherry and Jerry Stotter to his campfire. That left three other men sitting at the other one, wondering what was going on.

"It's pretty obvious we got somebody trailin' us," he told them. "I don't think Billy Boy and Dugan got killed by accident."

"Law?" Cherry asked. "Or bounty hunter?"

"That's what you're gonna find out, Del."

"Me?"

Caulfield nodded.

"First town we come to you're gonna go in and see what you can find out."

"How? Just ask?"

"Word travels fast," his cousin said. "Maybe you can even send a telegraph message back to Liberty."

"What if they ain't got one?"

"Like I said," Caulfield repeated, "word travels fast. You might hear somethin', or even read it in a newspaper."

"Why don't you send Jerry in?" Del asked.

"I can do it, Aaron," Stotter said.

"No," Caulfield said, "you might be recognized by somebody. I want Del to do it."

Cherry stared at his cousin for a few moments, then decided to go ahead and ask.

"This wouldn't be your way of gettin' rid of me, would it, Aaron? Like Leo and Otis?"

"No, Del," Caulfield said, "it isn't. We really do need this information. We gotta know who we're dealin' with."

"Next town is Bristow," Stotter told Del. "Telegraph key, lawman, newspaper. Everything you'll need."

"Just don't get caught," Aaron said, "and for chrissake, don't get yourself shot."

"I'll do my best."

"Now get some sleep."

"Sure."

But Del doubted he'd sleep all night.

"You startin' to be sorry you split us up?" Stotter asked.

"No," Caulfield said. "That had to be done. Besides, if we split up and there's a posse after us, then they had to split up, too."

"Good point."

"Go back to the others," Caulfield said. "Let them know we ain't cuttin' any of them loose."

"Okay."

As Jerry Stotter walked away, Caulfield thought to himself, Not yet, anyway.

As Stotter was passing, Del Cherry hissed at him and beckoned him over.

"Why ain't you asleep?"

"What do you think he's doin', Jerry?" Cherry asked.

"He's doin' what he wants," Stotter said. "He's the boss, remember?"

"Yeah, but we had a good thing goin', and he goes and splits us all up."

"Look, Del," Stotter said, "I don't care, okay? I do what I'm told, and that's what you got to do, too. Don't worry about it."

"Easy for you to say," Del said. "You got a rep. He wants to keep you around."

"Come on, Del—"

"Jesus, what if he wants to go straight? I can't go straight, Jerry, can you?"

"Just go to sleep, Del," Jerry Stotter said. "You got a job to do tomorrow."

TWENTY-SEVEN

The next morning, Clint saddled Eclipse and rode over to the sheriff's office. As promised, the man was there and he had a pot of coffee going, to boot.

"One cup, and then I'm on my way," Clint said.

"You know," the other man said, "in a way I envy you."

"Why?"

"It's excitin', what you're doin'," Anderson said. "Tracking down those killers. I wish I could sit a horse and go with you."

"You've probably got it best of all, Sheriff," Clint said. "A small, quiet town where people respect you, and no one wants to kill you because of some stupid reputation you never asked for."

Anderson frowned.

"Guess I never thought of it that way," he admitted.

"Just enjoy it while you can, Sheriff," Clint said. "Thanks for the coffee. I've got to be on my way."

Sheriff Anderson walked him outside.

"Longarm shows up, I'll send him your way," he promised.

"Much obliged, Sheriff," Clint said. "Take care."

• • •

Aaron Caulfield pointed to the town of Bristow.

"There it is. We'll keep on goin' and you can catch up to us, probably in a day."

"If I don't get killed," Del said.

"Don't get yourself killed, Del," Caulfield said. "That'd piss me off. I've already gotten rid of all the men I need to."

"Right, Aaron," Cherry said. "I'll collect the information and catch up."

The five men watched Cherry as he rode off toward Bristow.

"Think he'll get it done?" Stotter asked.

"How could he not?" Caulfield asked. "All he's got to do is get some information. Jesus, why's everybody makin' it out to be so goddamned hard?"

Caulfield turned his horse and headed in the opposite direction. The others followed, with Jerry Stotter bringing up the rear. Maybe it wouldn't sound so damned hard if all of Aaron Caulfield's relatives didn't seem so dumb.

Del Cherry rode into Bristow and immediately began looking for the newspaper office. If he found a paper with the information he needed quickly, he could get back on the trail soon.

As he reined in his horse a man wearing sleeve garters and a visor came out of the newspaper office.

"This your newspaper?" he shouted.

The man squinted up at him, moving his head so the visor blocked the sun.

"It is."

"You hear anything about a shooting in Liberty yesterday?"

"Liberty?" The man rubbed his jaw. "Ain't heard nothin', yet. Liberty's got their own paper, though."

"You get it here?"

"Sometimes," the man said, "but won't be for days."

"Liberty got a telegraph?"

"Yep."

"Got one here?"

"We sure do," the man said. "We're a growin' town."

Del looked around. Sure didn't look like a growing town to him, but then he'd never seen it before.

"Telegraph's up the street," the newspaperman said.

Del didn't bother to thank him, just gigged his horse and started up the street. But along the way, before he could get there, he passed the local whorehouse.

It was an hour later and Del Cherry was looking down at the gal who was sucking his dick. She was doing more than that, though—at the moment she had his rigid cock in her hand while her face was buried somewhere beneath his testicles. He felt her tongue on his asshole, lapping away like he crapped taffy, not turds. No wonder she charged so much. He'd never had a woman do this to him before.

She continued to lick him, working the length of his cock with her hands, then she ran her tongue over his balls, back up his shaft and took him into her mouth. She started to suck him wetly and he grabbed hold of her head as he felt the buildup in his legs and thighs.

"Jesus Christ, woman," he said. "Come on up here and sit on it so I can suck your titties."

She obliged him by letting his slick penis slide free of her mouth so she could mount him. She felt between them for him, grabbed hold, and stuffed him into her steamy pussy. He almost exploded right there and then but managed to hold off. Her huge tits swung down in front of his face and he grabbed them and started sucking on the thick nipples. She was forty if she was a day and her breasts probably weren't nearly as firm as they'd once been, but damn, this woman knew what to do to a man in bed! She was more than worth the extra dollar!

TWENTY-EIGHT

Clint wondered what possible reason Aaron Caulfield could have for taking his men into Utah? New Mexico, Arizona, he could understand. But Utah Territory?

He rode along, following the tracks the Caulfield gang had been leaving, wondering if maybe they were just passing through Utah on their way to Nevada. Nevada had some big ranches, owned by rich people, that the gang could hit.

Abruptly, he came across their campsite from the night before. Only two fires, since their numbers were dwindling. He walked the site on foot, saw that one set of tracks headed off alone while the others continued on. Had one of the men left the gang, or been sent on a mission of some kind? The tracks headed off in the direction of a town called Bristow.

Billy Boy, the man he'd caught in Liberty, had been useless. Apparently, Caulfield didn't talk about his plans with his men, so what would be the point of following the set of single tracks to Bristow?

He decided to just keep on heading west, on the trail of the six—no, it looked like five—riders who were still together.

Would Caulfield try to hit a ranch with five men? Or did

115

he intend to restock? Or were his intentions to start hitting other targets?

He mounted Eclipse and turned in the saddle to look behind him. He wondered what had happened with Longarm and the remainder of the gang. Surely, the lawman must have gotten close enough by now to determine that Caulfield wasn't with them. He should have turned around by now and headed back. Or was he so ego-driven that he'd just had to try to take those other members of the gang into custody?

Clint thought maybe he was being too hard on the deputy marshal. He'd been wearing a badge a long time. Maybe he was used to people doing what he told them to do. He sure did seem intent on doing his job, though. Couldn't fault the man for that.

He stopped looking behind him for Longarm and gigged Eclipse to move on. If Longarm caught up to him, fine. If not, he was now trailing about five men, and the odds seemed to keep growing—or shrinking—in his favor.

"He fucked it up."

Jerry Stotter looked at the man on the horse next to him.

"Maybe he fell into a bottle, Aaron," Stotter said. "Del likes his whiskey."

"And his women," Aaron Caulfield said. "He probably fell into a whore, too. If he passed a whorehouse—well, Del Cherry has never passed a whorehouse without goin' in."

"So we're down to five if he don't come back," Stotter said.

"That's okay," Caulfield said. "Five's plenty for what we got to do."

"So you do have a plan?" Stotter asked.

Caulfield looked at him. "I've always got a plan, Jerry. It just ain't my way to let on until I'm ready. You know that."

"Yeah, I know that, Aaron."

Stotter turned in his saddle to look behind him at the other three men.

"We keepin' them?" he asked.

"Yeah," Aaron said, "they're good boys. We'll keep 'em on for a while."

"So where we headed?" Stotter asked. "Someplace right here in Utah?"

"This territory don't hold nothin' for us, Jerry," Caulfield said. "We're just passin' through."

"Nevada, then?"

"Relax, Jerry," Caulfield said. "I'll let you know in time."

"So then, we ain't worried if somebody's followin' us?"

"We ain't that worried," Caulfield said, "but I'd still like to know, wouldn't you?"

"Yeah, I would."

"Let's stop in the next town, then," Caulfield said. "Maybe we'll send a telegram or two of our own."

TWENTY-NINE

When Clint came upon the ranch house, he thought it was a prime example of the kind of place the gang would hit. Not a huge spread, but well built enough to indicate that something more than dirt farmers lived there. Neither house, corral, nor the barn were in a state of disrepair. There were some horses in the corral that looked like good stock, but there were no hands in sight. In fact, the place looked too damned quiet. If not for the fact that the gang had burned every ranch they'd hit, he might have thought this one had already been hit.

But it hadn't and—since the gang's tracks led Clint right past here—that begged the question, Why?

Clint decided to take the time to ride down to the ranch and ask some questions. Maybe the gang had come by and been seen, maybe they'd even been fought off.

As he approached the house, though, there was no sign of any recent firefight activity. Certainly, if it had occurred there'd be chunks of the house gouged by flying lead.

He dismounted in front of the house and still no one appeared. He looped Eclipse's reins around a post and approached the door. He could hear the sound of children from inside, always a good sign. He knocked and waited.

119

The door was opened by a man in his late thirties, a pleasant if puzzled expression on his face.

"Hello, friend," he said.

"Hello," Clint said. "I was just passing by and—"

"Please," the man said, "come in and partake of our hospitality."

"Well . . . thanks."

He entered the house, the man stepping aside to let him do so, and then closing the door behind them. From his vantage point Clint could see both kitchen and sitting room, and doorways leading to other parts of the house. The sound of children was much clearer in here, and the smell of something delicious came from the stove.

"Mary, Rose, we have a guest!" the man called.

Clint assumed the man was calling his wife and daughter, but two grown women appeared. One was a handsome woman in her midthirties and the other a younger woman, pretty and in her twenties. From behind their skirts peeked several children.

"My name is James Harmon," the man said to Clint, "and these are my wives, Mary and Rose."

It took Clint a few seconds to process that the man had said "wives."

"Please, can we persuade you to share our table?"

"Well, I really just stopped to ask some questions—"

"Nonsense," Mary, the older woman said. "We were about to sit to supper. Surely you'll join us."

"We'll not take no for an answer," the pretty woman said.

"Well, in that case . . ."

"Excellent," James Harmon said. "Come, sit, I'll get you some coffee."

Before going for the coffee, though, the man went to the three children—a boy and two girls, all under eight, it seemed, with the boy being the oldest—and spoke to them in a low voice. The two girls turned and went deeper into the house, while the towheaded boy went outside.

"Eugene will see to your horse," James said.

"That's not nec—"

"He's very good with horses, really," James said. "He'll brush him and feed him."

"I may be riding again very soon," Clint said.

"It will be dark, soon," James said. "We insist you stay the night."

"We'll not take no for an answer," Mary said.

"Truly," Rose said.

Clint raised his hands helplessly and said, "Well, I guess I'm outnumbered."

"And what would your name be, friend?" James asked.

"It's . . . Clint."

"Clint," James said. "A strong name." They did not press him for his last name.

James sat down and one of his wives brought the coffee for the two men.

"And what brings you this way?"

By way of answer Clint took out the deputy marshal's badge and showed it to James.

"I'm tracking some men who rode this way," he said. "I was wondering if you saw them."

"You are the first guest we have had in weeks," James said.

"Well, these wouldn't be guests," Clint said. "These men are guilty of murders and . . . and worse."

"What could be worse?" Rose asked.

"Believe me, ma'am," Clint said, "there's worse."

"We have not seen any men of that nature," James said.

"Their tracks show they rode right by here, probably in the last day or two."

"Then perhaps we are fortunate they did not stop here," James said.

"If that's the case," Clint said, "then you are very fortunate, indeed."

"Supper is ready," Mary said. "Rose, would you get the girls?" She looked at Clint. "I hope you like beef stew."

"I love it," he said. "I haven't had a good hot meal in quite a while."

"Then, my friend," James said, "you are, indeed, the fortunate one, for my wives are excellent cooks."

Clint smiled and said, "I'm very glad to hear it."

THIRTY

Bad whiskey and a paid-for woman.

More often than not, those two things had combined to give Del Cherry trouble. This time, though, by the time he came to his senses he knew Aaron would kill him.

He left the whorehouse after two days, having spent most of his money. He went right to the hotel and got a room, then used a bath—which he hated—to try and sober up.

He hadn't gotten any of the information Aaron had sent him to get, so after the bath he was going to go and do that. If he could catch up to his cousin with the information maybe he wouldn't have to worry about getting killed. After all, they were family.

He was still in the bath, which had grown tepid, when suddenly the door to the room slammed open and a man stepped inside. He was tall, mustachioed and—worst of all—wearing a badge.

"Shit!" Del said.

"Get yourself out of the bathtub and dried off, old son," Longarm said. "We have some talking to do."

Clint had spent the night in the livery on another hay bed. James and his wives apologized, but they had no bed for him in the house. He told them their hospitality was appreciated.

They invited him inside for breakfast before he left. The ladies had set out a feast and insisted in replenishing his stores when it came to bacon and beans and coffee. He tried to pay them but they would not hear of it.

By the time he was ready to part company he was extremely happy that Aaron Caulfield and his gang had bypassed them.

But he was still puzzled about why.

"We're drifting south," Stotter said to Aaron Caulfield.

Aaron looked across the fire at Stotter and then said, "Yeah, we are, Jerry."

"Arizona?"

"That's where we're headed."

"What's waitin' for us there?" Stotter asked.

"The biggest score we ever made."

Stotter looked around camp and over at the three men sitting beside the other fire.

"We got enough to pull it off?"

"I've whittled us down to these five," Caulfield said. "You, me, and those three. Believe me, Jerry, I've got the men I want for this job."

Stotter rocked back on his heels. He decided not to ask any more questions. He was just happy that there was some apparent method to Aaron Caulfield's actions. He'd been starting to wonder.

After Clint left the Harmon ranch he couldn't help but continue to wonder why Caulfield would bypass such an easy score? Then it came to him. He already had his next job picked out. That's where he was heading. The only reason to pass up easy jobs was if he had something specific planned.

He also noticed something else while following the tracks left by the five men. They were now heading south-west instead of due west. Could they be going to Arizona? Or even beyond? And how much farther was he going to be committed to this hunt without Longarm along? What if the deputy had been injured going after the other half of the gang? Or, even worse, was dead?

Clint decided he needed some reassurance. He had to find a town with a telegraph so he could send word to Marshal Billy Vail about where he was. Maybe Vail would have some information about Longarm or, at least, some instructions for him.

For now, he continued to follow the trail left by Caulfield and his remaining men. At least he knew, thanks to Billy Boy, that he was on the right trail.

Aaron Caulfield and his men broke camp and by midday they were on the road into a town called Foley. On the way in they spotted telegraph poles, so they knew the town had at least one thing they wanted.

Once they were on the main street of Foley, Stotter spotted the newspaper office.

"See what you can find out," Caulfield said. "I'm going to the telegraph office."

"Right."

"Take the men with you," he said. "Keep them out of the saloon and out of trouble."

"Right," Stotter said again.

Aaron continued on until he saw the telegraph office. It was two doors down from the sheriff's office. He hesitated, then decided to rein in his horse even farther down the street and walk up to the office. That way he would not have to pass the lawman's office.

As he entered the telegraph office the clerk looked up and said, "Afternoon. Can I help you."

"Yeah," Aaron said, "maybe you can."

THIRTY-ONE

Clint was surprised that the trail left by the Caulfield gang rode right into the town called Foley. Why stop in a town now, unless it was to cover their tracks? Once he got on the road to Foley the tracks became harder to follow because they both crossed and were crossed by others. If the gang suspected they were being followed, then they were trying to hide their trail. Maybe Longarm could have picked their horses out from among all these other tracks, but Clint could not.

He had no choice but to ride into Foley and ask some questions. Somebody might have seen or heard something that would help him. If this was not the case, he was going to have to try to pick up their trail again someplace out of town—maybe south.

He was pleased that Foley had both a newspaper and a telegraph office. Either one might yield something helpful. The gang might even have come to this town for the same reason. Maybe Caulfield was looking for news of his other men.

Clint went to the telegraph office first. When he saw that it was only two doors down from the local law, he figured he'd stop there next, before going to the newspaper.

As he entered, the the young clerk said, "Afternoon. Can I help you?"

"Maybe you can," Clint said. "First I'd like to send a telegram to Denver."

"Sure thing," the young fellow said. "You want to write it out or dictate it?"

"I'll write it, thanks."

The man pushed a pencil and pad over to Clint, who composed something short and to the point for the man to send to Marshal Billy Vail in Denver.

"You gonna be around for a reply?" he asked after Clint had paid.

"I'll be in town a few hours, at best," Clint said. "If an answer comes in during that time take it over to the sheriff's office."

At the young man's surprised expression, Clint said, "Yes," and produced the badge again. "I'm a deputy U.S. marshal. I'll be checking in with him."

"Sheriff Gates?"

"I don't know his name, but yeah."

"Uh, Sheriff Gates ain't in his office."

"He's not? Then where is he?"

"He, uh, was killed yesterday, Marshal."

"Killed? How? By who?"

"He got hisself shot down by some strangers who came to town."

"Strangers? Tell me about them."

"Well, there was five of 'em. One of 'em came in here and sent a telegram."

"Did you keep a copy?"

"He wouldn't let me."

"Where did he send it to?"

"Someplace in Arizona," the man said.

"Where in Arizona?" Clint asked. "What town?"

"I don't recall—"

"Try," Clint said. "It's very important."

"To tell you the truth, I was kinda scared," the telegraph operator said. "I mean, this man was kinda scary, and then him gunnin' down the sheriff and all—"

"You got any deputies in town?"

"We had one."

"He dead, too?"

"No," the man said, "he quit after, uh, yesterday."

"Okay," Clint said, "look . . ." He thought a moment. "You got a newspaper here, right?"

"Yeah," the man said, "the *Sentinel*."

"Did they cover the killing?"

"Sure did, today's edition."

"You got one here?"

"Uh, no—"

"Okay. I'm going over to the newspaper to talk to the editor there. If I get a reply, bring it over there."

"Sure thing."

Clint started to leave.

"Marshal?"

"Yeah?"

"You, uh, know who that was who gunned down the sheriff?"

"I think I just might," he said, and left.

THIRTY-TWO

Clint entered the office of the *Sentinel* to the clatter of the press. A tall, slender man was standing in front of it as newspaper pages came gliding off it. Clint looked around. There was an office on the side but this man seemed to be the only person in the place. He was wondering how to get his attention without scaring him when the man turned, as if sensing someone else was in the room. Clint started to speak, but the man put his ink-stained finger to his lips and beckoned Clint to come with him. He walked past him and entered the office. Clint followed and the man closed the door. The clatter of the press decreased but just enough for them to talk.

"What can I do for you?"

"My name's Clint Adams," Clint shouted, and showed the man the deputy's badge. "I'd like to talk—"

The man waved him quiet again and then said loudly, "Just hold on. I'll stop the press so we can talk."

That suited Clint. He nodded and waited. When the man reentered he was holding a pad and a pencil.

"When I woke up this mornin'," he said, "I didn't think I was gonna get to interview the Gunsmith."

"Whoa, easy," Clint said. "I'm not here for an interview."

131

"When did you become a U.S. marshal?" the man asked. "I didn't know you were wearin' a badge—"

Clint reached out and snatched the paper and pencil from the man's hand.

"Hey!" the man said.

"I'm here to ask questions, not answer them," Clint said. "Are you the editor here?"

"Editor, owner, everything," the man said. "The name's Ebbett, Sam Ebbett."

"You can't be more than thirty."

"Twenty-eight," the man said, "but what's that got to do with anything?"

"Okay," Clint said. "Look, I'm here about the shooting yesterday."

The man's eyes widened. "Wow! Didn't take the government long to send in a deputy marshal, did it?"

"I'm here by coincidence, Mr. Ebbett," Clint said. "I've been trailing the men who shot the sheriff since they burned some ranches and killed some people near Denver."

"It was one man who gunned the sheriff," Ebbett said, "but yeah, he was here with a gang. Four or five other men."

"What about—"

"Look," Ebbett said, "I'm not gonna answer any more questions unless you do."

"Don't you want the man who killed your sheriff caught?"

"Putting aside the fact that Sheriff Gates was a pompous ass who got himself killed yesterday," Ebbett said, "yes, but what kind of a newspaperman would I be if I didn't take advantage of this situation? I mean, you're the Gunsmith, for chrissake."

Clint studied the man for a few moments, then said, "Yeah, okay." He returned the pad and pencil. "But me first."

"I got your word you'll answer some questions?"

"You've got my word."

"Okay, then."

According to Ebbett, the sheriff pressed and pressed the stranger who came to town yesterday until the man couldn't take it anymore.

"He finally drew and fired," the newspaperman said. "I think he just did it to shut Gates up."

"Did the sheriff know who he was?"

"Beats me," Ebbett said. "All I know is that the man shot him down on the street. Witnesses said Gates was following the man, shouting at him."

"What about the other men in the gang?"

"I can describe one of them real well."

"Why's that?"

"He was in here with me when the shooting happened."

"He give you his name?"

"No, but the other men waited outside, and one of them stuck his head inside and called the fella Jerry."

"Let me describe him. Real tall and thin, dresses in black, wears his gun on the left side."

"That's him. Who was he?"

"His name's Jerry Stotter."

"Gunman?"

"Yes."

"I knew it. I could tell just by lookin' at him."

"Did he go running out after the shooting?"

"Yeah," Ebbett said, "that's when one of the others stuck his head in to tell him that Aaron had—hey, I remembered a name. He said 'Aaron just shot the sheriff.' Aaron who?"

"Caulfield."

"Never heard of him."

"You wouldn't have, but you might have heard of Stotter."

"Come to think of it, now that you mention it . . ." He wrote the name down.

"Did they leave town after that?"

"No, not right after. They went to the General Store and got some supplies."

"Pay for them?"

"Why would they?" Ebbett asked. "Their leader had just killed our only law."

"I thought there was a deputy."

"Took his badge off real quick after that shooting. Can't say I much blamed him."

"I guess not. You didn't happen to see which way they went when they left town, did you?"

"Not me," the man said. "I was in here writing my story by then. You want to see it?"

"Anything in it you haven't already told me?"

"No."

"Then I don't need to see it."

"You wanna know anything else?"

"Not right now."

"Then it's my turn."

Clint frowned.

"You gave your word."

"Okay," Clint said, "okay, ask, but I'm only giving you ten minutes."

"That's fine," Ebbett said. "First, tell me how come you're wearing a deputy marshal's badge . . ."

By the time the newspaper editor–owner had finished with his interview, the door opened and the telegraph operator stuck his head in.

"I get an answer?" Clint asked.

"No, sir."

"Well, I'm going to get a drink and then move on," Clint said. "Anything comes in in the next fifteen minutes I'll be at the nearest saloon."

"That'd be the Grubstake," the operator said. "Right down the street."

"Okay."

"One more question—" Ebbett said, but Clint cut him off.

"We're done, Editor," he said. "I think we're even here."

Clint left the newspaper office with the telegraph man trailing behind him.

"Hey, mister."

"Yeah?" Clint turned.

"You said you wanted to know the name of the town that fella sent his telegram to."

"You remembered?"

"Sure did," the man said. "It was called Quincy."

"Quincy, Arizona?"

"Yes, sir."

"You're sure."

"Yes, sir."

Clint took out a dollar and handed it to the young man.

"Hey, thanks."

"I get a reply to that telegram in the next fifteen minutes—" he started.

"I'll run it right over to the saloon," the man finished for him. "Guaranteed."

"Okay, thanks."

"Thank you!"

As the man ran back to his office, Clint decided to retrieve Eclipse and walk him over to the saloon with him. There was no longer any hurry to have a quick beer. Not when he knew what town Aaron Caulfield was headed for.

THIRTY-THREE

Several days after the killing of Sheriff Gates in Foley, Aaron Caulfield, Jerry Stotter, and their three men rode within sight of the town of Quincy, Arizona.

"What's so special about this town that we came all this way, Aaron?" Stotter asked.

"It don't look special to you, Jerry?" Aaron asked.

"Hell, naw," Stotter said. "It looks like a million other towns I been to."

"Well, this town has somethin' those other ones didn't," Aaron told him.

"Yeah? Like what?"

Caulfield looked over at him and said, "This is where I'm from."

"What?"

"I was born here," Aaron Caulfield said.

"When's the last time you were back here?"

"I ain't been back since I left fifteen years ago."

"So why are we back now?"

"So I can do somethin' I been wantin' to do for a long time."

Stotter looked down at the town again. It still looked like a nothin' collection of buildings in a dust bowl.

"Is there money here for us, Aaron?"

"Don't worry, Jerry," Caulfield said. "There's somethin' here for all of us."

Stotter hoped so. He was starting to get tired of following Caulfield around with no immediate payoff in sight. And after what happened in Foley—Aaron gunning that lawman down for no good reason—Stotter was starting to run out of patience with the man.

"We goin' in?" he asked.

"Oh yeah," Caulfield said, "we're ridin' in." He turned in his saddle. "You three ride in first. Me and Jerry will follow."

The three men exchanged glances. They'd already seen most of their number discarded by Aaron Caulfield, including his own cousins. Was he now sending them on their way?

"Don't worry," Aaron said, "we'll be followin' you right in. I just don't want to attract a lot of attention by ridin' in together. Just ride in, get your animals taken care of, and get hotel rooms."

The three men hesitated only a moment more, then moved their horses past Caulfield and Stotter and headed into town.

"These folks gonna remember you, Aaron?" Stotter asked.

"I doubt it. We lived outside of town, kept to ourselves. Pa came in for supplies sometimes. I left when I got old enough, and before he could start puttin' me to work."

"How old were you when you left?"

"Fourteen."

Stotter thought he'd been working a long time by the time he'd turned fourteen. He also thought Aaron was a lot younger than he looked. His thinning hair made him look almost forty—Stotter's age. Now he felt silly, following and taking orders from somebody who wasn't even thirty yet.

"We ridin' in?" he asked.

"Give those three some time to get into town and put their horses up," Aaron said. "We got time."

Clint watched from his hotel room window as the three men rode into town. He had no way of knowing if they were riding with Caulfield or not. Once he'd found out about Quincy he'd been able to take a more direct route and—mostly because he was riding a superior horse like Eclipse—was pretty sure he'd arrived before Caulfield and his men. These were the first strangers to ride in since he'd set up shop in this hotel room day before yesterday.

There was a knock on the door as they rode right past his window.

"Come on in."

It opened and a pretty girl entered carrying a tray of food. When he took the room he'd arranged for his meals to be brought over from a café down the street. The girl's name was Carla, and she and her mother ran the restaurant.

"Here's your lunch, Clint."

"Put it down somewhere, Carla. Thanks."

Carla put the tray down, then stood with her hands clasped behind her back, her young breasts thrust forward. At seventeen she was as fresh and pretty as a girl could be, and she was fascinated by Clint. She'd been throwing herself at him for two days and he wasn't about to catch her. Not a girl that young.

"Is there anything else I can do for you?" she asked.

"Not right now, Carla."

"You sure?"

Curiosity made him take his eyes from the window. Carla had her hand on her skirt, raising it up so he could see her thighs. She was also wearing a low-cut peasant blouse, which showed off young breasts the size of peaches.

"Cut that out, Carla," he said. "You're going to give me a heart attack."

"You ain't that old."

"Too old for you," he said. "I keep telling you that."

"I think you could handle me just fine," she said. "I think you and me could have some fun right here on this bed, right now."

"And if I was ten years younger I'd take you up on that offer," he said. "But if your mother found out about this she'd come looking for me with a shotgun."

"You can't be afraid of my mother," she said.

"You bet I can, and I am," he told her. "Now you get on back to work. She's going to be wondering where you are."

She dropped the hem of her skirt.

"I'll go back to work," she said, "but the time is gonna come, Clint Adams, when I won't offer myself to you anymore. Then you'll be sorry." She stamped her foot for emphasis and huffed out the door.

He was already sorry, but she was just too damned young.

THIRTY-FOUR

Caulfield's three men did as they were told, but slightly changed the order. They put their horses up in the livery, then went to the saloon for a drink, and only then did they go to the hotel and get two rooms. After that it was just a matter of staying out of trouble, and waiting.

Aaron gave his men an hour to get to town and get settled, then said to Stotter, "Okay, let's go."

Stotter had waited the entire hour in silence, formulating a plan in his head. At the end of the hour he knew what his plans were for himself, depending on what happened in and around the town of Quincy over the next day or so.

Aaron Caulfield's thoughts only went to a certain point. After he achieved a goal he had set for himself, he didn't really know what was going to happened to him, and he didn't care what happened to his men, his cousins, or to Jerry Stotter.

Upon arrival in Quincy, Clint had sent another telegraph to Denver to Marshal Billy Vail, telling him where he was and what his plans were. Vail still had no word on Longarm's condition or whereabouts. Clint thought that there were is-

sues going on between Longarm and Billy Vail that he
didn't know about and didn't want to know about.

He had made a decision for himself, though. Quincy
was as far as he was going to go with this. If the issue
didn't resolve itself here, if he didn't catch Aaron Caulfield
right here, he wasn't going to try to track the man any farther. He'd taken this assignment temporarily, and tempo-
rary it was going to be. He didn't intend to give any more
of his time to it after Quincy. That would be Deputy Marshal Custis Long's job and, failing that, any other deputy
Billy Vail managed to hire and send after Aaron Caulfield.

After this he was done carrying the deputy marshal's
badge in his pocket.

He had seen the three men who had ridden into town go
into the saloon across the street. Apparently, they'd put
their horses up at the livery, intending to stay awhile.
Armed with only a description of Aaron Caulfield—a description curiously devoid of anything that would make the
man stand out at first glance—he remained at the window.
The only time he left the window was to relieve himself, or
after dark to go to bed. By first light, though, he'd be back
at it.

After he'd sent the telegram to Denver, his next move
had been to talk to the local sheriff. Quincy was a town that
had reached its full potential years ago. Part of that potential was a town sheriff and one deputy. The sheriff, a
portly, mustachioed man with a perpetual pained look on
his face, was seated behind his desk when Clint entered. In
his fifties, he'd certainly lived long enough to have earned
whatever pain was etched on his face.

"Sheriff," he'd greeted the man.

The sheriff had shifted in his seat with a wince—
indicating part of the problem might have been a pain his
butt—and asked, "Sheriff Dan Bartle. What can I do fer ya?"

Clint told the sheriff his name and showed the man the

badge. The sheriff acted unimpressed by both. He listened while Clint spoke to him about Aaron Caulfield and his gang, all the while continuing to shift in his chair. At one point Clint realized the man was sitting on a pillow. Another man who'd had all the years in the saddle he was going to have.

When Clint was done, the sheriff said, "Never heard of him."

"How long have you been sheriff here?"

"Nine years."

"So you can't think of any reason this man might be coming here? A bank, maybe? A rich rancher in the area?"

"We got none of that," Sheriff Bartle said. "I can't imagine why someone would ride all that way to get here. Wouldn't be here myself if I didn't have to be."

"Well, I just wanted to let you know I'll be in town for a while."

"Waitin' on your man?"

"That's right."

"I don't want no lead flyin' in my streets, Adams," Bartle said. "I don't need no innocent people gettin' killed."

"I'll do my best, Sheriff," Clint promised. "If you need me I'll be at the nearest hotel."

The sheriff shifted in his chair and said, "I doubt if I'll need you, but if I do I'll send my deputy for ya."

"Fair enough."

Two days and no deputy had shown up, which suited Clint. He hadn't done anything to put himself in trouble with the local law, anyway. But he wondered now if he could get the sheriff—or his deputy—to check out the three strangers who had just ridden in.

He'd finished his food, so he wouldn't be seeing anyone until someone came for this tray and brought him another.

Then maybe he could send a message over to the sheriff's office.

Clint had allowed himself to relax at the window, but right at that moment he sat up straight. Two men were riding down the street, and he thought he recognized one of them.

THIRTY-FIVE

It was dusk as Aaron Caulfield and Jerry Stotter rode into Quincy, Arizona. The street was quiet, almost empty. Aaron looked around, noticing that not much had changed since the day he'd left.

Stotter kept waiting for somebody to recognize Aaron. He didn't understand why Aaron wouldn't expect it, even after fourteen years. Somebody had to be left behind from that time. Still, even if someone did recognize him, Aaron was probably not wanted in Arizona, and his reputation had probably not spread this far.

Stotter, on the other hand, always expected to be recognized, and then challenged. It was a way of life for men like him—men like Hickok and Earp, Bat Masterson and the Gunsmith. Stotter didn't kid himself that his reputation was equal to theirs, but with a gun he felt he was the equal of any man, and the better of most.

They managed to ride down the main street to the livery without anyone running out and pointing at them, without anyone recognizing either one of them.

Or so he thought.

• • •

Clint leaned forward, then back. He did not want to be spotted in the window. One of the men fit Aaron Caulfield's description, but a lot of men would have. It was the other man he recognized as Jerry Stotter. He'd only seen Stotter once or twice, and was surprised that he'd recognized him immediately.

And if that man was Jerry Stotter, then the other had to be Aaron Caulfield.

Now the problem was that Caulfield was not wanted in Arizona. And as far as Clint knew, Stotter was not wanted anywhere. The man was a gunman, but he'd never heard that he was a cold-blooded killer.

And he didn't have a federal warrant for Caulfield. If one existed, maybe Longarm had it, but he'd never mentioned it.

He had options. He could run down right at that moment and brace them, before they joined up with the other three. But to stop them in the street would mean gunplay. Clint was confident in his ability with a gun, but he wasn't stupid. He'd never seen Jerry Stotter's move, but had heard that he was very good with a gun. And he'd heard it from people he respected. To rush into a confrontation would have been foolish. And there was still the chance that Longarm would show up. When they'd left Denver they'd known that there was a possible two against fifteen, or sixteen, showdown coming. Now there was a possible one against five, or two against five. The odds, in either case, had improved dramatically since leaving Denver. But the plan had been to try to get Caulfield away from his gang and take him, and that was still a viable option.

Clint decided there was no rush. The first three men had taken hotel rooms, and it seemed apparent that Caulfield and Stotter were on their way to the livery. Hotel rooms were logically next. If they were staying in town, even overnight, there was no urgency to face them.

He watched and waited and, sure enough, the two men

returned on foot, carrying rifles and saddlebags, and went into the hotel across the street. It was a little more than pure luck they had not chosen the same hotel he was in. He'd purposely chosen the more run-down of the two, hoping that men like Caulfield and Stotter would choose the better of the two.

It was dark when a knock came at the door and he knew his supper had arrived.

"Come in."

This time the woman who entered with the tray was older, in her late thirties. She was a more mature, much lovelier version of Carla, her daughter. Her name was Diana.

"Here's your supper, Clint," she said.

He turned away from the window, stood up, and stretched. "Thanks, Diana."

"You're stiff from sitting there all day," she said. "Sit back down and I'll rub your shoulders."

"I won't turn that offer down."

He sat back down and she came up behind him and put her hands on his shoulders. As she rubbed and kneaded he could feel the heat of her body through her simple blouse, the fullness of her breasts pressing every so often against him.

"Your daughter threw herself at me again today," he said.

"That hussy," she said. "I assume you turned her down."

"I did. I'm a responsible gentleman, you know."

"Yes, I do know." She squeezed his shoulders hard. "You better be. That's my baby."

"Some baby," he said. "You're lucky it's me she's throwing herself at. Any other man would catch her."

"Not you, huh?"

He turned quickly, slipping his arms around her waist.

"Now why would I want to catch the daughter when I've already caught the mother?"

"Some men would take that as a challenge," she said, looking down at him.

"I take my challenges one at a time," he told her, nuzzling her through her blouse. Her breasts were large, the big nipples evident beneath the fabric.

"Some challenge," she said, lazily, "you had my legs in the air the first time I came up here."

"Seemed like a good idea at the time," he said. "In fact, it seems like a good idea now."

THIRTY-SIX

Clint peeled Diana's clothes from her and pulled her close, pressing his face into her warm cleavage, and cupping her full buttocks. Her dark nipples hardened as he nibbled on them. She smelled of fried foods, perspiration, and sex. At that moment it was a headier concoction than if she had just come from a bath. Clint loved everything about how women smelled.

She leaned down to kiss him then, hungrily thrusting her tongue into his mouth. The room was filled with the sounds of their kissing for a while, and then he stood and backed her up to the bed. She sat on it and undid his belt, and before long his pants were off and she was on her knees in front of him, sucking him wetly. He held her head lightly as she slid him in and out of her mouth, then she released him and continued to undress him until he was as naked as she was.

They fell onto the bed together with him on top, his rigid penis trapped between them.

"Ooh, God," she groaned as he kissed her neck and shoulders. "Carla would kill us if she saw us. She wants you so bad."

He kissed her, bit her bottom lip, and said, "If you were a good, loving mother you'd share."

She slapped his ass soundly and said, "Bite you tongue."

"I'd much rather bite yours," he said, and did.

Aaron Caulfield registered in the hotel for his own room, as did Jerry Stotter. He noticed on the register that his other men had taken two rooms for the three of them.

The desk clerk handed each of them their keys and said, "One and two, top of the stairs."

Aaron took his key without a word.

"Where's the best steak in town?" Stotter asked.

"Down the street, Diana's Café. Best food in town."

"Thanks."

They went up the stairs together and stopped in front of their rooms, which were across from each other.

"You wanna get a steak?" Stotter asked.

"Yeah, sure," Aaron said. "Let's just drop off our gear. I'm starvin'."

"What about the others?" Stotter asked.

"As long as they stay out of trouble we don't need to find them until mornin'," Aaron said. "Nothin's gonna happen until then."

"Fine," Stotter said. He unlocked his door, tossed in his saddlebags, but retained his rifle. "Let's eat."

Clint rolled Diana over so she was lying on her stomach, big breasts flattened beneath her. He moved her long dark hair out of the way so he could kiss the back of her neck, then moved his lips down the line of her back, sending shivers through her. He then kissed the swell of her butt, running his tongue along the crack between the two luscious moons. He spread her legs, then reached between them to slide his finger along her moist portal. She gasped when his finger entered her, then twitched when he inserted another. She was so wet she was soaking the sheet beneath her.

He controlled her now, completely. Gripping her by the hips he got her up on her knees and slipped between her legs to kneel right behind her. Parting her thighs he slid his rigid penis up between them and entered her cleanly. She gasped and pressed her butt up against him, taking him in deeply. He began to slide in and out of her that way, gripping her hips, increasing the tempo so that the sound of slapping flesh on flesh filled the air. Every time her butt came back and banged into him it sent ripples through the flesh of her butt. She began to sweat now, moisture mixing with moisture, the entire room starting to smell like sex. As he slammed into her faster and faster his own sweat began to drip off the point of his chin. An open window would have helped, but he wasn't about to stop what he was doing. And even if he'd wanted to, he didn't think she'd let him.

Stotter eyed the cute waitress as she brought over their steaks.

"Hope they're okay," the girl said. "My ma's the regular cook, but she ain't around right now."

"They look fine, darlin'," Stotter said. He put his hand on her ass, feeling how firm it was until she moved away. He figured that as a waitress she was used to being pawed. Probably liked it.

"Bring some more coffee, will ya?" Aaron Caulfield asked her.

"Sure thing."

As she left he leaned forward and said, "Stop touchin' the girl, Jerry."

"What's it to you, Aaron?"

"I wanna eat in peace."

"Yeah," Stotter said, with a grin, "I wanna eat a piece, too."

"They got whorehouses for that."

"I bet there ain't nothin' as fresh and sweet as her in any whorehouse."

"Your steak's gettin' cold."

Stotter looked down at his plate and suddenly realized how hungry he was.

"Yeah, right," he said. He cut off a hunk of meat and stuffed it into his mouth. It bled into his plate, which meant it was prepared perfect for him. When the girl came back with the coffee he left her alone.

For now.

THIRTY-SEVEN

"Now I have to go back to work smelling like a goat," Diana complained.

"You smell great," he said, watching her from the bed as she got up and moved around the room.

"For a bedroom, maybe," she said, "but not for a restaurant—not even to a man. I'm gonna use your water and basin."

"Be my guest."

Naked, she poured water from the pitcher to the basin, then started wetting a cloth. She looked over her shoulder at him.

"Are you gonna watch me?"

"I am," he said, putting his hands behind his head.

"Okay," she said, "but you stay on that bed. I have to get back to work."

"No promises."

His penis was limp as she started washing, but as she used the cloth to clean under arms and breasts, and then between her legs, he started to harden again. By the time she was done he was at full mast.

When she turned and saw him she said, "Bastard."

"I can't help myself."

She walked to the bed, her eyes on his hardness, and said, "Neither can I."

She leaned over and took him fully into her mouth. As she rode him with her mouth she moaned and held the base of his cock with one hand. The other hand she ran over his chest and belly. He kept his hands behind his head and watched her as she worked him with her mouth and her hands until finally he couldn't hold it back. He lifted his hips and exploded in her mouth with a gutteral cry. . . .

By the time they got to dessert, Jerry Stotter's interest in the waitress had been revived.

"Do you have to do that?" Aaron asked.

The girl had put a slice of pie in front of each of them and had quickly sidestepped Stotter's roaming hands.

"Aaron," Stotter said, "I've seen you rape a dead woman. What's your problem?"

"Maybe it's that this one is still alive."

"And you only like dead ones?"

"I don't think she likes what you're doin', is all."

"Well, too bad. I like live, warm women," Stotter said, "and you know what? They don't have to be willing, either."

"Now I really have to go," Diana said, wiping her mouth with the same damp rag.

"Suit yourself."

He watched with pleasure as she got dressed, and was semihard again by the time she finished.

"No," she said to his penis, "you'll just have to wait."

However, she did walk to the bed, lean down, and kiss him, lingering over his lips with her tongue.

"You are the wettest woman," he told her, "in more ways than one."

She looked at the soaked sheets and said, "It's you fault. No man's ever made me gush like that before."

"Stop," he said. "Just hearing that word come out of your mouth is getting me going again."

"Well," she said, moving to the door, "you're both just gonna have to wait until I close up later tonight."

"I'll be here," he said.

She pointed to the tray of food she'd brought him and said, "Eat it. Even cold it's good. I'm that good a cook."

"I know it."

She smiled at him, took the tray from earlier in the day, and left. He wondered what kind of story she was going to tell Carla.

When Diana reentered the café, she saw that there was only one table occupied, by two men. They were on dessert, so apparently Carla had done all right with them. She smiled at the men and went into the kitchen.

"Where have you been?" Carla demanded.

"I got held up—"

"That big, mean-looking one keeps putting his hands on me," the young girl complained.

"Is that a fact?"

"I think I should go get Clint to shoot him!"

"That won't be necessary," her mother told her. "Have you given them their check yet?"

"No," Carla said. "I didn't want to go back out."

"I'll do it," Diana said.

"Are you sure I shouldn't get Clint?"

"I can handle these two," Diana said. "Give me their check."

Carla handed it over. Diana took it, then went to a corner of the kitchen, opened a box, and took out a small .32 Colt, which she was able to hide beneath the folds of her skirt.

"I'll handle this," she said, and left the kitchen.

THIRTY-EIGHT

Clint woke the next morning to the sound of someone hammering on his door. He rolled to his feet, grabbed his gun, and held it down by his side while he answered.

"Clint, you gotta come quick," Carla said, grabbing his hand.

"What is it?"

"It's my ma," Carla said. "She's at the doc's."

"What's the matter with your ma?"

"Some man beat her up last night."

"What? Last night? Why didn't you come and get me then?"

"She wouldn't let me," Carla said, yanking on his arm, "but you gotta come now."

"All right, all right," he said, "but let me get dressed. I'll be right with you."

"Don't close the door."

"I have to close the door to get—"

"I don't wanna be out here alone. Please?"

"All right," he said. "Come in while I get dressed."

For a moment he thought this might be another ploy of hers to get into his room while he was naked, but while he dressed she barely looked at him, dispelling that theory.

When he was finally dressed he strapped on his gun and said, "Okay, let's go."

The doctor was an older man named Gentry, and he explained to Clint what had happened, as he was able to piece the story together from Carla and Diana Simms.

"Apparently, Carla was in the café alone and two men came in. She waited on them, but one of them insisted on putting his hands on her every chance he got. When Diana came back, Carla told her mother what was going on. Diana went to the table with their check in one hand and a gun in the other. The short of it is she told them never to come back and showed them her gun."

"And?"

"One of the men took it away from her and pistol-whipped her with it," Gentry said.

"How bad?"

"Opened up one side of her head pretty good," the doc said. "I bandaged it, and I'm hoping there's no brain damage."

"Is she awake?"

"She was," Gentry said, "but now she's asleep—or in a coma."

"You can't tell?"

"I'm just a country doctor, Mr. Adams," Gentry said. "If she wakes up soon I think she'll be okay."

"Why didn't you send for me last night?"

"You'll excuse me, but I didn't know anything about you or your connection to these two until Carla told me this morning. Apparently, once Carla realized her mother wasn't sleeping a normal sleep she decided to go and get you. I don't know what she thinks you can do for her mother that I can't."

"I think you do, Doc."

"Well," Gentry said, "that's going to be between you and your conscience—and the sheriff."

"Thanks, Doc. Can I see her?"

"She won't even know you're there," Gentry said. "I prefer you just wait."

"Okay."

He went outside, where Carla was waiting for him.

"What are we gonna do, Clint?" she asked.

"We're going to wait for your mother to wake up, Carla," Clint said. "The doc's doing all he can, and there's nothing I can do to help her."

"What about the two men?"

"That," he said, "I can do something about. All you've got to do is describe them to me."

THIRTY-NINE

Clint was angry enough to track down Aaron Caulfield and Jerry Stotter and brace them immediately—especially Stotter, since it was he who had pistol-whipped Diana. But he was carrying a badge and he decided to take Carla over to the sheriff's office and let her tell her story to Sheriff Bartle.

The sheriff listened to her, then looked at Clint.

"These are the men you been trackin'?"

"Yes."

"This Stotter, he's a money gun?"

"Yes."

"Fast?"

"Very."

"Well, I tell you, Adams," Bartle said, "I ain't very fast and if I go up against this money gun, I'm gonna end up dead." He looked at Carla. "Little lady, I'm gonna leave this up to Mr. Adams here, who just happens to be carryin' a deputy marshal's badge."

"You're not gonna do anything?" Carla asked.

"I'm gonna do what I just done told you I'm gonna do."

"But you're the sheriff."

"I'm a live sheriff," Bartle said, "and I wanna stay that way."

"Come on, Carla," Clint said. "We're not going to get any help here."

Outside, on the boardwalk in front of the sheriff's office, she asked "Are you gonna kill them, Clint?"

"I'm going to make them pay for what they did to your mother, Carla," Clint said.

"You gonna go over there and shoot them?"

"Carla," he said, "what you don't know is that there are five of them altogether. So I've got to figure out a way to do this. What I need you to do is go and stay with your mother."

"But—"

"I can't do a thing if I'm worried about you," he said. "I need to know you and your mother are off the streets. Do you understand?"

"I understand," she said. "You'll come and tell me when it's over?"

"You'll be the first to know," he promised.

As she walked away he thought to himself, but I'll have to be alive to tell you.

Clint took up a position across from the hotel that Caulfield and his men were in. He was waiting to see if they were going to leave the hotel for breakfast, and if so, if they were going to be all together. He was hoping to catch Caulfield alone, but that wasn't to be. The other three men came out and walked down the street. There was still no proof they were with Caulfield and Stotter, but Clint felt sure they were.

A few minutes later, both Aaron Caulfield and Jerry Stotter came out together. They stopped in front of the hotel and exchanged a few words, then turned and walked in the opposite direction of the other three men. Still no proof they were together.

Clint got up from the chair he was sitting in and followed along, staying on his side of the street. Finally, the two men went into a restaurant and got a table away from the window. Clint waited until he was sure they'd be settled in, and then entered and approached their table.

"Wha—" Aaron Caulfield said as Clint sat down, but Clint cut him off before he could get any further.

"Thought I'd join you boys for breakfast," he said, grabbing the coffeepot from the table, and the empty cup from in front of Caulfield.

"Who the hell are you?"

Clint looked at Stotter.

"Why don't you tell him, Jerry?"

Caulfield looked at Stotter.

"You know him?"

Stotter studied Clint for a few moments.

"It'll come to you," Clint said.

And it did. Stotter's face lit up as recognition dawned.

"Clint Adams."

"That's right," Clint said.

"The Gunsmith?" Caulfield asked.

"Right again."

Aaron looked at Stotter.

"You two friends?"

Stotter shook his head. "Ain't friends. Just acquaintances."

"What do you want?" Caulfield demanded.

"I want you boys."

"For what?"

"Well," Clint said, "for one thing, murder in Colorado. And for another . . ." He looked at Stotter. "I want you for what you did to a woman last night."

"Smart-ass woman," Stotter said. "She a friend of yours?"

"She is."

"She deserved what she got," Stotter said. "You tell her I said so."

"No," Clint replied. "I'd rather tell you that, Jerry. You deserve what you're going to get."

"What do you want here, Adams?" Caulfield asked.

"Oh," Clint said, "I forgot to tell you."

He took the badge from his pocket and dropped it on the table.

"Aaron Caulfield, you're coming back to Denver with me to stand trial for murder."

Caulfield looked at Stotter.

"And what about me?" the gunman asked.

"I was going to bring you back, too," Clint said. "But after last night, I think I'll just kill you. It'll be difficult enough to get him back to Colorado. I'd rather not try to bring both of you back."

"And where are you gonna kill me, Adams?" Stotter asked. "In here?"

Clint looked around at the other people in the restaurant.

"No," he said. "I can wait, Jerry." He stood up. "I just wanted to let you both know what was going to happen."

He turned to walk away.

"Hey, Adams," Caulfield said, "you forgot your badge."

Clint stopped, turned, and came back.

"Oh yeah," he said, picking up the badge. "Thanks."

He started away again, then stopped and returned of his own accord.

"One other thing."

"What's that?" Caulfield asked.

"The other three men you've got with you?"

"Yeah?"

"Tell them to stay out of my way."

"I'll tell 'em," Aaron Caulfield said, "but I doubt they'll do it. You're gonna have to take the five of us."

"That's your choice," Clint said, "and theirs."

"I think," Caulfield said, "you're gonna have to get by Jerry here, first, and I don't think you can do it."

Clint and Stotter exchanged looks.

"Well then, I guess that'll be his choice."

With that, Clint turned and left.

"Whataya think?" Stotter asked. "Should I go out and take him?"

"I've got something to do first," Caulfield said, "and then we'll take care of him."

"We?"

"I'll back your play, Jerry," Caulfield said. "I think you can take him, but I'll back your play, and so will the other boys."

Stotter nodded.

"Don't you think you can take him?"

"Oh yeah," Stotter said. "I can take him."

"It'll be a big feather in your cap," Aaron said. "You'll be the man who killed the Gunsmith."

Stotter thought that that alone would be worth all the bullshit he'd put up with from Aaron Caulfield for the last several months.

FORTY

Caulfield had Stotter go out and round up the other three men.

"Do you even know their names?" Stotter asked.

"What?"

"You always say 'the other three,'" Stotter said. "You don't know their names, do you?"

"What's the difference?"

Stotter thought a moment, then shrugged and said, "I'll round 'em up."

"Take 'em over to the livery and saddle our horses," Caulfield said. "We're gonna take a ride."

Jerry Stotter and the other three men followed Caulfield out of town for about an hour until they came to a ranch house.

"What the hell—" Stotter said.

The house was run-down, the front door off its hinges, the glass on the windows broken out. Tumbleweed rolled through the back door and out the front. The corral was half collapsed, and the same could be said for the barn.

"What are we doin' here?" Stotter asked.

The other three men wondered the same thing, but didn't have the balls to ask.

Caulfield dismounted.

"We're gonna burn it down."

"Why?" Stotter asked. "There's nothin' here."

Caulfield looked at the other men.

"Dismount, look around, find me something that will burn. Wood, cloth, something that will make a good torch."

They obeyed, but Stotter remained in the saddle.

"Jerry."

"What's goin' on, Aaron?"

"I told you," Caulfield said, "I'm burnin' this place to the ground."

"Why?"

"This is where I was born," Caulfield said, "where I grew up, the place I left fifteen years ago."

"And now we're back why? Is there money hidden nearby? We're gonna dig it up?"

"No," Caulfield said. "I'm just gonna burn it down. It's time."

Stotter looked into Caulfield's eyes and saw something he'd either never seen before, or something he had never wanted to see.

"You're crazy."

"You might be right."

"I'm leavin', Aaron," Stotter said. "I've wasted a helluva lot of time on you."

"You made money."

"You said there was a big score in our future," Stotter said, "but that's not true, is it?"

"Could be."

"Well, I'm not gonna wait around to find out," Stotter said. "I got me a Gunsmith to kill back in town, and then I'm outta here."

"Suit yourself, Jerry," Caulfield said. "I've got my—I've got these other men . . ."

"Whose names you don't even know." Stotter shook his head. "Wait 'til they figure it out, Aaron."

"Get out, Jerry," Caulfield said. "I don't need you any-more."

"No," Stotter said, "it's me who don't need you any-more, Aaron."

Stotter turned his horse and started back to town. Aaron turned and looked at the house he had been born in.

Clint watched Caulfield, Stotter, and the other three men ride out of town. They did not have their saddlebags on their horses, which meant they weren't leaving town for good. He decided to give them a little bit of a head start and then track them to see what they were up to. If they were going to hit a nearby ranch he was going to have to act alone. He already knew he'd have to take Stotter first, and then Caulfield if he had any hope of taking all five of them.

He was saddling Eclipse at the livery when he heard a horse ride in. He turned and looked up at Longarm, who was mounted on a dun.

"What took you so long?" he asked.

"I had a problem or two. Where's Caulfield?"

"I'm riding out to get him right now," Clint said. "Want to come along?"

"I wouldn't miss it."

Jerry Stotter heard two horses coming up the road toward him. He directed his horse behind some bushes to allow the riders to pass by. As they passed he saw that one was Clint Adams, and the other was another man wearing a badge.

Stotter decided to just go to town and wait for Clint Adams to return.

FORTY-ONE

". . . they decided to hit this ranch, so I rode down ahead of them to warn them. Guess what I found?"

"What?"

"Four brothers and a sister, all of whom could use a gun," Longarm said. "When the eight of them came riding in— including two of Caulfield's cousins—we blasted them."

"I'll bet they were surprised."

"Extremely."

"And where've you been since then?"

"Tracking you."

"Me? Not them?"

"You," Longarm said. "I found another Caulfield cousin, Del Cherry, in a town called Bristow. He didn't have much to tell me, so I left him in the care of the local law and started tracking again. After Foley, I was tracking you instead of them. Your horse has a very distinctive gait."

"If you were tracking me why didn't you get here sooner?" Clint asked.

"My horse stepped in a chuck hole. Took me a while walking and carrying my saddle before I came across a ranch that would sell me one. Look, don't complain. I'm here. How many men we got to face?"

"Five, including Caulfield and Jerry Stotter."

"Stotter?"

"A gun for hire."

"You know him?"

"Slightly, but we had a run-in early today."

Clint told Longarm about Diana and what Stotter had done to her. By the time he was finished with the story they could see the smoke.

"Shit," Clint said. "They must've hit already."

They both urged their horses into a dead gallop.

By the time they reached the source of the fire the building was completely engulfed in flames. Caulfield and three other men were about to torch the barn.

"Something's wrong," Clint said. "This place is abandoned. Why would they torch an abandoned ranch?"

"Why don't we ask them?" Longarm asked. "Four against two. The odds have evened up a lot."

"Your call," Clint said.

Longarm stepped out from cover and Clint followed.

"Aaron Caulfield!" the deputy shouted.

Caulfield turned, as did his men, to watch as Longarm and Clint approached,

"Another deputy?" Caulfield asked Clint.

"He's a real deputy," Clint said. "I'm just helping out."

"Drop the torches, boys," Longarm told the others.

They all looked at Caulfield, who said, "Drop 'em."

The torches all struck the ground.

"Now your guns," Longarm said.

"Oh, no," Caulfield said. "Those you'll have to take."

"You're all under arrest."

Caulfield laughed.

"Are we just supposed to throw up our hands?"

"Preferably," Longarm said. "I really don't want to have to kill you."

"Where's Stotter?" Clint asked.

"He left," Caulfield said. "Quit me. I don't need him. I got all I need right here."

Clint knew Caulfield was referring to the burning house, not the other three men.

"So let's go," Caulfield said. "I'm ready."

"You men ready to die with him?" Clint asked.

"They ain't ready to go back to Denver to hang," Caulfield said. "So let's do it."

Clint could see the uncertainty in the eyes of the three men. Given a little more time he felt they could have been talked into surrendering, but Aaron Caulfield did not give any of them that time. He went for his gun, and started a chain reaction of lead and death.

FORTY-TWO

Clint and Longarm had the same idea—to take Caulfield out first. Clint's bullet struck him in the chest, followed by Longarm's slug, which hit him in the belly. Because they had both fired at the same man, they were in danger from the other three, who had all followed Caulfield's example and drawn their guns.

Clint reacted first. He dove and clipped Longarm behind the knees, causing the man's long legs to fold just as the three men fired. Hot lead went over Clint's and Longarm's heads. Both men rolled—Clint right, Longarm left—and came to a stop with their guns blazing. Longarm's bullets hit one man, dropping him to the ground, while Clint fired economically, one slug for each man.

Clint and Longarm got to their feet with their guns ready, just in case Jerry Stotter was still around. Longarm walked over to the fallen men to check and make sure they were dead while Clint covered him.

Satisfied that all four were dead, both men ejected their spent shells and began reloading.

"I owe you," Longarm said. "You saved my life."

"Guess we should have had a plan," Clint said. "Who shoots who first."

"It worked out." Longarm holstered his gun. "Now, where's Stotter?"

"He's got to be back in town, waiting."

"For what?"

"For me."

"Why would he be waiting for you?"

"I told him I was going to kill him for what he did to Diana."

"The waitress?"

"The owner of the café."

"You and she got . . . close?"

"We're friends."

"Okay, then. Go."

"What?"

"Go and take care of it," Longarm said. "I'm gonna get these four tied to their horses and bring them in. You make contact with the local law?"

"Yeah," Clint said, "sort of."

"Okay," the deputy said. "I expect you'll be done by the time I get to town."

"If I'm dead," Clint said, "he'll be waiting for you."

"You won't be dead."

"What makes you so sure?"

"I ain't sure," Longarm said. "I'm hoping. I mean, if he kills you, chances are real good he'll kill me. So, to avoid that, you kill him. Okay?"

"Hey," Clint said, "that works for me."

FORTY-THREE

When Clint rode into town he could feel something was wrong. What he hoped he was feeling was the possible absence of tension in the air. Maybe Jerry Stotter had decided to leave town. Maybe that's what he was feeling—but he doubted it. What he was feeling was bad, very bad.

He reined in Eclipse right in front of the sheriff's office, but when he tried the door it was locked. He decided to go over to Doc Gentry's office and see how Diana was doing. He was approaching the office, keeping an eye out for Stotter the whole time. He wouldn't have put it past the man to ambush him from a rooftop, although he'd really thought the man was looking forward to trying him face-to-face.

As he reached the doctor's office he was surprised when the door burst open, and even more surprised when Carla Simms came out—with Jerry Stotter right behind her.

Stotter had one arm across her chest, and his gun in his other hand.

"Hold it right there, Adams," he said.

"I didn't expect this from you, Jerry," Clint said. "This is the act of a coward."

"This is the act of a careful man," Stotter said. "Where's that other deputy? The one I saw you ridin' with?"

"He's out collecting bodies," Clint said. "Aaron Caulfield and those other three."

Stotter looked up and down the street carefully.

"Nobody's with you?"

"It's just you and me, Stotter," Clint said. "I thought that was the way you wanted it?"

"That's just the way I want it, Adams," Stotter said, stepping into the street with Carla. "I just want to make sure."

"Clint?" Carla said, her voice trembling.

"Don't worry, Carla," he said to her. "He's going to let you go soon."

"I'm gonna let her go, all right," Stotter said, "but only until I kill you. Then me and her are gonna get real well acquainted. Ain't we, honey?" He moved his hand so that he was cupping one breast, squeezing hard enough to make Carla wince.

"Okay, let her go, Jerry," Clint said. "You got what you want. I'm right here. Unless you want to hide behind her all day."

Stotter took Carla into the center of the street with him, still tightly holding on to one breast.

"I don't need to hide behind her, Adams," Stotter said. "Like I told ya, I'm just makin' sure."

"Well, are you sure now?"

"Yeah," Stotter said, "yeah, I'm sure. I just want a little taste before I let her go."

With that he licked the side of Carla's face, then turned her and pushed her away so hard she stumbled and fell in the street. Now that she was free she hurriedly wiped his saliva from her face with her hand, as if it were burning her.

"Come on, Gunsmith," Stotter said. "You've had it your way for too long. It's time somebody put you facedown in the street."

"It's been tried by better men than you, Jerry," Clint said. "Men who'd think that pistol-whipping a woman was the act of a coward."

"That's what this is about?" Stotter asked. "Not the fact that you're wearin' a badge?"

"I'm not wearing a badge now," Clint said. "This is just between you and me."

"I wouldn't have it any other way."

As he spoke, his hand streaked for his gun. Clint watched, impressed with the man's move. He was as fast as they said he was—almost.

In fact, Jerry Stotter almost had his gun up when Clint shot him. The bullet struck him in the chest and caused him to pull the trigger of his own gun, discharging it into the street. His mouth opened but no sound came out, then he stumbled to his knees. He tried to bring the gun up again, but couldn't. Before Clint could decide what to do—fire again or simply approach—Carla was on her feet. She ran at Jerry Stotter and launched a kick that caught him right in the jaw. His eyes rolled up into his head and he fell onto his back. His gun fell from his lifeless hand.

Clint approached quickly and kicked the gun away, just in case.

"Is he dead?" Carla asked, anxiously.

Clint leaned over, then straightened.

"Yeah, he's dead, Carla."

"Did I kill him?"

"No," Clint said, "no, I did that."

She looked at Clint, her chest heaving as she breathed heavily.

"I wish I'd killed him," she said, and then spat on the body.

"No," Clint said, "no you don't. Tell me, how's your mother?"

"She—she was just waking up when he came in and grabbed me. I think she's gonna be okay."

"Well," he said, putting his arm around her, "why don't we go and make sure, huh?"

FORTY-FOUR

Clint walked into Diana's Café a couple of days later and found Longarm seated there waiting for him. He stuck his head into the kitchen and saw both mother and daughter there. Diana still had a bandage on the side of her head, but she was much better than she had been.

"Go and sit with your friend," she said. "Steak and eggs are comin' out."

Clint smiled, withdrew, and went to join Longarm at his table. Of the seven or eight tables in the place, only about three were being used at the moment. He and Longarm were sitting out of earshot of the other two, which appeared to be occupied by town merchants.

"Mornin'," Longarm said. "Coffee?"

"Absolutely."

The deputy poured him a cup and handed it to him.

"How did you sleep?" Clint asked.

"Like a log."

Clint doubted that. He'd heard the commotion coming from the deputy's room and was sure that Carla had finally thrown herself at somebody who had caught her. If she was anything like her mother, the man hadn't gotten a good night's sleep at all.

Clint had slept well. Although her injury did not keep Diana from coming to his room, all they had done was cuddle and sleep together.

"I got a reply from Billy Vail in Denver," Longarm told him. "He's very happy with the outcome."

"With most of the gang dead or in custody, I would think he would be."

"He'd like me to bring you back to Denver," Longarm went on. "Seems we still don't have enough deputies and—"

"Oh, no," Clint said. He hurriedly removed the badge from his pocket and set it down on the table. "You take that back with you. I'm done being a deputy."

"That's what I thought you'd say." Custis Long picked up the badge and put it in his own shirt pocket.

"I was just supposed to make sure you didn't get killed," Clint said.

"Well, you did that and I'm much obliged, old son," Longarm said.

Both Diana and Carla appeared then, each laden with plates of food that they set down in front of the two men.

"Enjoy, gentlemen," Diana said. "It's on the house."

As she turned to go back to the kitchen, Carla bumped Longarm's shoulder with her hip and said, "That's not all that's on the house," confirming Clint's suspicions about last night.

"When are you heading back?" he asked the deputy.

"As soon as I finish this breakfast."

"Carla's going to be disappointed."

"I've got to get back to work," Longarm said. "What about you? When are you on your way?"

"Same thing," Clint said. "As soon as we finish."

"Which way are you headed?"

"East," Clint said. "I'm heading for Texas."

"I'm goin' northeast," Longarm said. "Headin' straight back to Denver."

"Looks like our days of ridin' together are over," Clint said.

"Looks like it."

Both men applied themselves to the feast that was before them, each keeping it to himself that he felt no real displeasure at the prospect of heading their separate ways.

Watch for

THE KILLING BLOW

301st novel in the exciting GUNSMITH series
from Jove

Coming in January!

GIANT ACTION! GIANT ADVENTURE!

THE GUNSMITH

GIANT

Giant Westerns featuring The Gunsmith

Little Sureshot and the Wild West Show
0-515-13851-7

Dead Weight
0-515-14028-7

Available in October 2006:
Red Mountain
0-515-14206-9

Available wherever books are sold or at
penguin.com

J799

J. R. ROBERTS

THE GUNSMITH

Penguin Group (USA) Online

What will you be reading tomorrow?

Tom Clancy, Patricia Cornwell, W.E.B. Griffin,
Nora Roberts, William Gibson, Robin Cook,
Brian Jacques, Catherine Coulter, Stephen King,
Dean Koontz, Ken Follett, Clive Cussler,
Eric Jerome Dickey, John Sandford,
Terry McMillan, Sue Monk Kidd, Amy Tan,
John Berendt…

You'll find them all at
penguin.com

*Read excerpts and newsletters,
find tour schedules and reading group guides,
and enter contests.*

Subscribe to Penguin Group (USA) newsletters
and get an exclusive inside look
at exciting new titles and the authors you love
long before everyone else does.

PENGUIN GROUP (USA)
us.penguingroup.com